A

'Is there something you're not telling me?' Alex said, aware that her voice was rising. 'There is, isn't there? Is Harry ill?'

No answer.

'Roger this is ridiculous!' Alex burst out. 'What are you trying to do to me? What is the matter?'

'Well I suppose Harry *is* kind of ill,' Roger said puffing out his heavy moustache. 'At least I think he is.'

His words seemed to galvanize Emma, who moved quickly over to Alex. She tried to take her hand, but Alex kept them both firmly clasped in front of her, her figure upright.

'We think Harry's had some sort of breakdown, darling. Please sit down and try and relax. He's really quite all right . . .'

'Is he in hospital?'

'No no. It's not that sort of breakdown. Sort of emotional really. *Please* sit down, Alex.'

Alex sat down on the sofa, her hands still clasped stiffly in front of her. She was aware that her heart was beating regularly and slowly but very loudly, so that surely they would both be able to hear it.

By the same author
**available from Mandarin Paperbacks*

*A Woman's Place (*as Katherine Yorke*)
The Perfect Wife and Mother (*as Nicola Thorne*)
The People of the Parish
The Girls
In Love
Bridie Climbing
The Daughters of the House
Where the Rivers Meet
Affairs of Love
The Enchantress Saga
Champagne
Pride of Place

The Askham Chronicles

Never Such Innocence
Yesterday's Promises
Bright Morning
A Place in the Sun

Nicola Thorne

A Woman Like Us

A Mandarin Paperback

A WOMAN LIKE US

First published in Great Britain 1979
by William Heinemann Ltd
This edition published 1990
by Mandarin Paperbacks
an imprint of Reed Consumer Books Ltd
Michelin House, 81 Fulham Road, London SW3 6RB
and Auckland, Melbourne, Singapore and Toronto

Reprinted 1994

A CIP catalogue record for this book
is available from the British Library
ISBN 0 7493 0236 4

Printed and bound in Great Britain
by Cox & Wyman Ltd, Reading, Berks

For Carole Ottaway

Part One

Alexandra

1

It was a day that started so well, Alex always remembered, a day on which she strolled around the garden after the children had gone to school cutting off the dead heads of the roses. She remembered it was a fine clear autumn day with the leaves shading from ochre to burnt red, and from the small park in the crescent came the pungent, nostalgic smell of wood smoke.

Alex had seldom recalled such a positive feeling of happiness as she had that day, a deep-down contentment, a sense that all was well and would stay well. A pleasure in herself, in her home, in the things about her as she'd made the beds and washed up the breakfast dishes; and then with secateurs she'd sauntered out through the french windows of the sitting room into the garden where more pleasure lay. She had created the order and symmetry of the garden from an abandoned wilderness which she and Harry had found, as well as a house badly in need of redecoration and repair, when they moved into Bonnington Crescent in the third year of their marriage, just before Rachel was born.

The house had seemed unbelievable after such a short time of living in a third floor flat. But Harry's father had died just as she became pregnant with Rachel, and he'd made them promise to spend the money he was going to leave them on a fine house with plenty of room so that they could extend their family quite comfortably to the four they'd wanted, and have Harry's mother to live with them too.

So they'd bought the large detached Victorian house pleasantly situated facing a small private park. It had huge windows and ornamental stone friezes which were now painted white like the woodwork, while the rest of the outside was an attractive shade of pink. The garden Alex had fashioned over the years, and the basement had been converted into a self-contained flat with its own entrance for Harry's mother.

Everyone had said how lucky Harry and Alex were to have so quickly what most couples took a long time to achieve, and fortunate too in Harry's mother, a sweet non-interfering person who took care of herself but was always available for baby-sitting. In fact, Alex and Harry Twentyman had been happy for years and, on this particular day, this mellow golden autumn day, Alex was more aware of it than usual. She snipped the heads off the roses and thought that autumn was a comfortable, anticipatory time – a season of large fires, frosty breath and warm stews, a preparation for the winter as one stocked up the pantry and freezer rather as squirrels buried their nuts.

Of course the Twentymans had their share of trouble – which couple didn't? But from what she heard they seemed to have fewer than most. They had the usual colds and chills, the usual alarms about the children's health from time to time; Harry's nasty appendix operation; the occasional business crisis when government taxes or the grape harvests affected Harry's small wine firm. But even the continental harvests in the seventies had been almost uniformly good, not like the sixties when some years – '65 and '68 for instance – had been almost disastrous. And then there had been the inevitable sadness when Harry's gentle mother had died, with commendable speed, from viral pneumonia.

Yes, most people envied the lifestyle of the Twentymans, except some said you couldn't possibly be so happy, there must be *something* wrong. Perhaps Harry's job was really too much of a strain, or Alex's domestic life very boring, or perhaps, just hopefully, they didn't have a very good time in bed. And then those children, they were too good to be true. Attractive to look at, open, honest, fun-loving, full of life – there had to be something wrong somewhere. For instance, take Alex's expression of almost constant good humour, wasn't her smile a little too frequent, too protracted? Or Harry's infectious air of *bonhomie* – perhaps he drank too much, it was a risk in his business? No, there had to be something wrong; some deep misery in the Twentyman household they were at pains to conceal. Everyone had them after all. No one had the right to be happy all the time.

That day, Alex remembered, she had gardened almost until noon and then gone for a swim in the baths at Swiss Cottage. It was the quietest time of day. There were just a few lazy people like herself idly swimming up and down the long length of the Adelaide pool or making little practice dives from the lowest board.

After the swim she'd shopped at Sainsbury's because Harry was coming back that night and she wanted a special French cut of roti de luxe from their continental meat counter to welcome him home. It had been a wonderful year for wine and Harry would be happy with his purchases. She'd already stood up a bottle of the '66 Clos de Vougeot to have with the beef. Harry always appreciated the care Alex had taken to interest herself in wine, to be knowledgeable about it, to know what to serve with what. And over the years she'd taken as much trouble to become an excellent cook too, gourmet standard, and if it wasn't true to say of every man that the way to his heart was through his stomach, in the case of Harry it certainly was. To start with that night they were having chilled mackerel mousse and a bottle of the crisp Beaujolais Blanc that had been a discovery of Harry's two years before.

No wonder Alex was happy, Harry coming back after two weeks abroad. What a welcome the children would give him, and she . . . well she often thought that Harry's frequent absences made them still appreciate each other so much in bed. Lying on her back in the pool, eyes blinking against the sunlight, she had quite deliberately and carnally looked forward to the love-making she and Harry were going to enjoy that night after the smoked mackerel mousse and the roti de luxe. Harry was sure to be pretty desperate after such a long time away.

Alex parked the car outside the house – like most London houses built in Victorian times theirs was without a garage – and took all her purchases inside. She just had time for a cup of tea before picking Rachel up from the convent. Toby was big enough now to come home from his school on his own. Today he was playing football and staying at a friend's house for tea. Alex was collecting Portia Drax, Rachel's best friend, and bringing her home for tea. Then Emma Drax, Alex's close friend and Portia's mother, was coming at six before driving to the airport to pick up Harry and her husband Roger. As well as being in business together Harry and Roger were old friends. It did seem a curious and fortunate coincidence how fond all the Draxes and Twentymans were of one another.

Alex looked in the pantry at the things she had made the previous night for the girls' tea. Then she larded the roti de boeuf with garlic, peppered it and put it on a wooden board a judicious distance away from the fairy cakes she had made for tea. She sniffed the mackerel mousse, gently prodding it with the tip of her very clean forefinger to make sure it wasn't too hard, or too soft, and checked that the white Beaujolais was chilling nicely on the stone floor. That was the advantage of an old house, the space and the convenient things like large cool pantries and the cellar for Harry's wine.

At three-thirty she left the house having drunk tea out of one of her beautiful porcelain cups and sampled a fairy cake. She got into her car for the ten minute drive to the exclusive and expensive convent where she and Harry had decided their daughter would receive the best kind of all-round education despite the fact that they were not Catholics. Not only would the teaching be of the highest standard, but she would be sure to learn nice manners too, the sort of thing that stood one in good stead throughout life.

Outside the school was the usual throng of mothers, most of them standing near or beside the middle range kind of car that Alex drove, usually rather sporty affairs in bright colours with drop-back hoods. The mothers mostly wore jeans or casually expensive sporty garb bought from the many casually expensive boutiques that proliferated in the high streets of Hampstead and St John's Wood.

After Rachel's three years at the school Alex knew all the mothers in her daughter's class and many more. There were frequent mutual tea invitations and the hours between three-thirty and six most week days were a hectic to-ing and fro-ing of children between large houses or spacious flats in the better parts of North London.

Alex was a bit late and Portia and Rachel were already on the pavement dressed in their neat brown and yellow uniforms, swinging their brown satchels. When they saw Alex's red Triumph sports swing round the corner they gave whoops of joy and ran towards her almost before she had time to stop. She leaned out smiling to receive Rachel's kiss, a peck on the cheek from Portia, before she got out to lower the front seat and let them into the back.

'Alex!'

Alex turned at the friendly greeting and saw Natasha Pont coming towards her, tailed by two small daughters and with the latest baby tucked head first under her arm. Natasha, married to an enormously wealthy stockbroker, had three elder children and a toddler somewhere between the diminutive girls and the baby. But she maintained an air of unravaged cheerfulness which maybe came of unquestioning acceptance of the will of God because the babies continued to come and, as far as anyone could see, would forever more, Natasha, a devout Catholic, being scarcely in her thirties.

'Alex can you and Harry . . .'

Natasha was waving a diary with her free hand. The Ponts were among the six or seven couples connected with the school with whom Harry and Alex exchanged dinner invitations, twice a year or so, not more. But it maintained a nice friendly link, a feeling of togetherness, of wealth, success and culture shared that was supplemented by the mothers meeting more often and exchanging invitations to tea.

'Oh Natasha! Harry's still in France. Not back until this evening . . .'

'Let's see about a date. Or would you rather leave it?'

'May I? Talk about it tomorrow? I'll have to see how Harry's fixed.'

'Of course, dear. Aren't you a lucky girl, having him back!'

Natasha winked; she knew all about those rapturous reunions that followed Harry's business jaunts. Alex acknowledged the wink with a shy smile and waved as Natasha crammed the children into her tiny orange Volkswagen and jolted off in a cloud of very black smoke which illegally poured from a broken exhaust.

'Mummy, can we go to the park?'

'*May* we, darling. You can, but the question is will I let you?'

'Oh Mum, say yes.'

Rachel was an instantly appealing child with melting eyes and a will of iron. Harry found it almost impossible to refuse her anything, yet Alex over-corrected by picking on Rachel and trying to discipline her whenever she could. She knew her remark was pedantic, and would be ignored by Rachel anyway and not even understood by the slightly obtuse Portia; yet she felt she had to make it just so that everything would not always appear so easy to Rachel.

'Well we can go to our park, not Regent's,' Alex said.

'Oh Mummy!'

'Darling, remember Daddy and Uncle Roger are coming home. Auntie Emma will soon be here too.'

'Yippee!' the girls yelled and spontaneously hugged each other. Yes, everyone was very happy. Roger and Harry had met in the City as young businessmen in the same large wine firm. They were both unmarried, but Harry and Alex knew each other and were practically engaged. By the time they married, Roger, who was Harry's best man, had met Emma and then Harry had been best man at Roger's wedding. Eventually Roger and Harry – with the money Harry's father had left, there had been a lot of it – had gone into business together as Twentyman and Drax Ltd, Wine Merchants.

It had taken Alex some time to like Emma, the product of a fashionable girls' public school and Oxford. In the early days Emma had been rather acid and unapproachable, as though in implied condemnation of Roger for her having to get married so quickly so as to make Portia legitimate, and thus forfeiting her own hopes of a career. Emma was defensive and at the same time rather aggressive and Alex, who had felt way out of her depth with her, had only made the effort for Harry; but she used rather to dread the compulsory annual holiday to Majorca or the south of Spain and the many social evenings the Twentymans and Draxes spent in each other's company.

Then Emma went into a clinical depression which lasted for some time but from which she eventually emerged hooked on analysis, prone to pill-taking, but a rather softer, gentler person – not so brittle, more understanding and, well, slightly more human. Although she still often made Alex feel her mental inferior, and Alex was quite happy to admit she was, the two got on well enough and rang each other for a chat several times a week.

Despite their age the little girls still liked childish things and they clung squealing to the roundabout or went higher and higher on the swings. Alex sat and watched them, smoking a cigarette and sniffing those fine autumnal smells, a hint of fog and the smoke which still rose from the pile of dead twigs and leaves in the corner near the summer house. The trees in the park were yellow-gold and overhead the misty sky of late afternoon had that pale pink tinge of approaching winter. Alex gave a sudden shiver of apprehension as she thought of fog descending on the airport, blanketing it out, delaying Harry's plane, diverting it to somewhere awful like Gatwick which would mean that Harry night not be home that night.

No. Fog had not been forecast. When Alex wanted something badly it seemed inevitable that she always dreamed up some awful reason why she wouldn't get it; it was as though a part of her was seeking to deny herself the happiness which was inevitable too, which was complementary to her well spent and well ordered life. She smiled to herself. No it was not time for fog, just a little autumn mist – 'season of mists and mellow fruitfulness . . .'

Fruitfulness. Alex had always wanted to have more children. Harry and she had actually agreed on four in those halcyon years at the beginning of their marriage when the fact of their fecundity had seemed like a biological cornucopia, a symbol of plenty, an invitation to people the earth with their own likeness. But this creative urge diminished in Harry when the chance came to start his business and multiply in that way; lots of pounds and pence overflowing instead of wet nappies and little booties. He said he could afford neither the money nor the time for another child and, because he added the word 'yet' Alex had obediently acquiesced because she was confident that Harry's urge to breed was as powerful as her own and, besides, a little gap between two was quite a nice idea.

But the gap was too wide. Even if she got pregnant today the baby would be nine years younger than Rachel. It would be like having two distinct families, and would definitely mean a little brother or sister would have to follow very soon after. Besides everyone said it was silly, maybe dangerous, to stay too long on the Pill. Alex would talk to Harry soon. Maybe tonight.

Alex shivered again, she had sat too long; it was getting cold and dark. She huddled into her coat and called the girls who gave the usual squalls of protest and started chasing each other round the small fenced-off playground.

But Alex couldn't be cross with them; she was too mellow, too content, too secure. Too happy in the knowledge that Harry would soon be home and their rounded, contented life together would resume its normal pace, at least until late winter or early spring when Harry's business would summon him abroad again.

2

Emma Drax stopped by at six on her way to the airport bringing with her Portia's night clothes. Emma had had her hair freshly done and wore an outfit which Alex didn't recognize – a sort of flowing one piece green silk trouser suit, that reminded her of one of those television advertisements for a new brand of Turkish Delight.

Not that Emma was blessed, or cursed, according to one's point of view, with the voluptuousness of an habituée of a Turkish harem. Never pretty, she was nevertheless good-looking, small framed and small in stature. She gave the impression of always being extremely busy, making up for her loss of physical height by generating an intense amount of nervous energy. Emma was a restless person to be with, lacking in what Harry's mother used to call 'repose'. She walked rather than sat, ran rather than walked and was most happy tearing around in her own small sports car being late for every appointment.

Tonight she both looked and smelt good and her hands dazzled with the size and variety of rings that Roger had plied her with over the years as though to atone for his many infidelities. Everyone knew Roger had other women; even Emma knew after all this time. He was a very tall handsome man with presence, dark eyes, flashing teeth, a heavy black moustache and smooth hair which appeared to be lacquered across his brow in a decidedly military fashion like a toy soldier. One could imagine the blonde, not very pretty but good-looking and clever Emma, conscious of her academic brilliance rather than looks, being a pushover for someone like Roger all those years ago.

Alex thought it astonishing that Emma stayed with Roger, never mind just tolerating his affairs. Emma talked about them a good deal as though the latest girl were one of the family, or a friend of whom she was especially fond. Because of her closeness to Harry, her trust in him, Alex found the Drax marriage almost impossible to comprehend.

As soon as Emma came into the house she started talking, and here she was now prattling away leaning against the kitchen table nursing a gin and tonic, apparently quite happy to let Alex get the children's tea, put them to bed and cook a gourmet dinner for four. Alex had neither changed nor thought what she was going to wear; it had taken her half an hour to scoop out the potato balls for *pommes parisiennes.*

'The table looks heaven,' Emma commented gazing through the glass doors to the dining area. Placed conveniently between the kitchen and sitting room, in summer this formed a patio which opened out on to a terrace, enabling barbecues or romantic dinner parties to be taken out of doors. Over the years the Twentymans had almost gutted the house, rebuilding it in stages, extending this and changing that with a degree of skill and imagination that excited the admiration of all who came, so that at least the first few minutes of new visits were spent in admiring the house.

Harry's mother had left them some fine linen and silver but, above all, a number of valuable pieces of antique furniture to which Alex and Harry had added their own collection, so that the style of the furnishing was mainly Georgian mixed with some of the better moments of Victoriana. The only modern furniture in the house was in the children's bedrooms and, of course, the kitchen, which was fitted with all the latest gadgetry too. Harry and Alex had a large mid-Victorian double bed with tall brass rails. On a solid oak tallboy stood a Wedgwood washbasin and jug which was entirely ornamental, the jug usually full of flowers because their modern bathroom adjoined and made washing in a basin quite unnecessary.

Alex had a flair for furnishing and decoration just as she had a flair for transforming a wilderness of weeds, high grass and tree stumps into a pretty garden. She loved flower-arranging and imaginatively-filled bowls, tubs and vases were attractively placed throughout the house to enhance the impression of gracious living. Alex had made her home her hobby; much of the paintwork, the minutiae of design she had done herself.

She felt it her function and her pleasure to complement Harry, the tycoon, the man of action, by providing him with a beautiful setting in which to find ease, to entertain his friends, to come home to.

That night Alex had set the table with one of Harry's mother's delicate lace German cloths so that the polished mahogany with an intricate blond marquetry in the wood, was shown in its gleaming perfection. The heavy Georgian silver and crystal glasses reflected the low lights from the sitting room on the other side. The thick wax candles in the sconces were primed, a taper with a box of matches lying near them on the table. The wine was ready to be decanted, resting on the sideboard at room temperature, and the mousse and white Beaujolais were in the dark pantry ready to be served. The potatoes were half cooked waiting to go into the hot fat with the joint, and the other vegetables were peeled and scraped anticipating the boiling water to be poured on them at exactly the right time.

The cheeses were in the dining room alongside the wine, their consistency perfect, the Brie not too firm but not runny and the blue veins of the Dolcelatte, a favourite of Harry's, glistening succulently.

The children were in the morning room finishing their tea, and Toby was due to be delivered back at the house by seven.

Alex was rather flushed.

'You do things exquisitely, Alex. Everything is such perfection. It always is.'

Emma lit a cigarette and blew the smoke away from Alex as she looked at her with admiration.

'I think I'll have a drink too,' Alex said, taking a cigarette from Emma. 'I usually don't until Harry comes home.'

'Don't you ever drink when Harry's away?'

Alex smiled because Emma sounded slightly shocked.

'Oh yes. I don't practise abstinence in everything. I mean when Harry isn't abroad I like to wait until he gets home and have a drink with him.'

'This has seemed a long trip.'

'I know. I feel all pent-up about seeing Harry, like a little girl. It's excitement.'

Emma glanced at Alex and turned away, stubbing out

her cigarette.

'I'm glad you get excited about something. You're always so cool.'

'Oh Emma, what a cruel thing to say. Untrue too.'

'Well to me you're always cool. "Poise" is what I say when I think of Alex; poised and cool and reflective. Everything is considered, Alex, isn't it? Under control?'

'It's the way I am. Is it dull?'

'Oh not dull. Enviable. I wish I had half your poise to calm me down a bit.'

As though to show how impossible Emma's wish would be she simultaneously looked at her watch, cried 'oh my God!', gathered her fur, gloves, scrabbled for car keys in her overloaded bag and rushed for the door.

'Look at the time. The *time.*'

'Ring me from the airport so that I can time the vegetables?'

'Of course.'

Alex saw Emma to the door and into the car, a half smile on her lips. She would find Emma's life impossible; it was like a cat trying perpetually to catch its tail. She went slowly back into the sitting room where she glanced at her face in the mirror – still pretty, she knew, young-looking, vital. An attractive woman.

She had known all these things about herself for years without being vain. She was a sensible middle-class girl; but all her life people had told her she was pretty, some said beautiful, and even as a tiny child she remembered people staring.

She was bright at school, but her ambition was never to go to university or a college of higher education. She wanted to work for a year or so and then get married. She knew exactly what she wanted to do and she did it. She took a secretarial course, almost immediately got a good job and at 19 was the personable secretary to the marketing-manager of the large firm of wine merchants where she met Harry.

Harry was just what she had visualized for herself – tall, accomplished, attractive, extrovert, fun to be with. Six years older than she, he'd taken a short-term commission in the Navy and this nautical tang, this jaunty nonchalance had remained with Harry ever since. His effortless sophistication was just the thing for a self-possessed young girl so ready to learn. It took them very little time to fall in love, and each set of parents approved the other's choice. Harry and Alex were so right for each other.

And so it had remained.

Alex tidied the sitting room – Emma invariably left an untidy trail wherever she went – and called the girls for their bath. They were both so excited about seeing their fathers again. Rachel was especially close to Harry and her dark animated face, so like Harry's too, was flushed.

'Oh I can't *wait*, Mummy, can you? Will he come up and see me?'

'I expect so, darling.'

She bent and kissed the eager little face, it was so irresistible, dark curly hair like Harry's, moist now on her brow, and dark brown eyes. Rachel was small, petite; she would not be tall and elegant like her mother, but fragile like a ballet dancer and indeed she was showing an aptitude for the ballet already, fastidious and agile on her feet. Harry's mother had been like that. Rachel very much took after Harry's side of the family.

On the other hand Toby, her beloved Toby, resembled her. He came in just as she was putting finishing touches to things in the kitchen, bluff and rumbustious and kissed her cheek.

'Hi Mum!'

'You're filthy, darling,' she cried backing away in mock alarm. 'Didn't you clean up at the Becketts?'

'Yah we did, imagine *what* we were like before!'

Toby always had the right answer, never obsequious but seldom cheeky; it was possible to converse with him like an adult. He had grown up with seeming effortlessness from a nice baby into a nice little boy, not special or extraordinary, but nice; a happy child. Like Alex he was fair and tall, but thickset, big for his age. An embryonic rugby player.

'What time will Dad be home, Mum?'

Toby was kicking off his boots into the middle of the kitchen floor, but Alex pushed him to the porch inside the back door.

'About nine.'

'Can I stay up?'

'I'd rather you were in bed. He'll come up and see you.'

'Will you tell him about the football on Saturday?'

'Football?' Alex consulted the kitchen board where she kept

notes of all the family's fixtures and appointments. 'Ah yes, against St Austin's. I'm sure Daddy will come if he can. We'll all come if you like. A family gathering.'

Alex smiled at him, prepared to make the sacrifice because she knew it would please him. She hated football.

'Oh Mum, that will be *great*!'

Toby, impulsive and affectionate, came up and hugged her.

'Get your bath now darling. Use our bathroom. The girls are in yours. Then come down and get your supper in the morning room.'

Toby clattered away and Alex turned back to the stove. She was trying to do everything now so that she would appear poised and relaxed when they arrived. She still felt hot. She was too excited about Harry and nervous about the meal. Ridiculous of Emma to say she was always cool. Emma meant 'cold' really; she was being bitchy. She liked to insinuate that Alex was frigid because Alex refused to discuss her sex life with anyone, let alone Emma who would tell half a dozen other people immediately. Anyway, Alex didn't need to discuss her sex life with anyone but Harry; and he knew perfectly well she wasn't frigid. She gave a little smile of contentment as she got on with the preparations.

* * *

The hour after the girls were coaxed into bed and Toby settled with a book went very slowly for Alex. Eight o'clock to nine. Everything was ready. She had dressed carefully, a straight long black dress with winged sleeves, a heavy gathered neckline from which folds fell in the front caught at the waist with a thin gold belt. She knew that Harry found the dress sexy and she wanted to please Harry that night.

She'd missed the nine o'clock news. Perhaps there had been a crash; that apprehension in the park was a premonition. She had to have something to do.

'Mummy, is Daddy home yet?'

Weary little voice from Rachel's bedroom. She steeled herself to keep her voice pleasant and calm.

'No darling, not yet. Go to sleep, girls.'

She tucked them up, kissing each one. Really Portia was getting very fat. It was spoiling her prettiness. She'd been Rachel's best friend for ages now, a tubby, friendly little girl, prone to giggles, the opposite of the beautiful rather supercilious Rachel in every way. For if Rachel had none of her mother's looks, she had inherited her temperament; for one so young she very rarely betrayed what she felt.

'But Daddy *always* brings . . .'

'Darling he'll give you your present, if he has one, in the morning. Sleep now, baby.'

Rachel grunted and Alex turned off the light.

Half past nine. There must have been a crash. The beef sizzling away in the oven would be ruined. Of course he was going to crash, to die after she'd been so happy all day; that intense feeling of happiness had really been rather unusual, the prelude to disaster obviously. She consulted the telephone directory, and dialled the airport. She must know . . .

The flight from Paris was not only in but had arrived early. All passengers had been cleared a long time ago, she was informed by a voice as calm as her own. Thank you.

It was selfish of Emma not to ring; but typical. She had probably been late at the airport. Maybe the men had gone for a drink and missed her. Alex felt a rare irrational rage. She wanted a drink. No, in that case she wouldn't have one. It was like losing control. If you always felt you needed a drink when you got upset, goodness knows where you would stop. She drank for pleasure not out of need.

She'd have to turn the beef off; the wine had been decanted too early and Harry would be able to tell.

A quarter to ten. Alex was aware of a sort of internal trembling, a very unpleasant feeling. The plane had landed an hour and a half ago. Even Toby's light was out. There was no possible reason . . .

A car crash! Of course. They had crashed over that awful flyover on the way from the airport. She closed her eyes and could see the car falling into the busy road below. Something had happened.

The bell rang. The bell! Harry had his key. Why hadn't he let them in? The police . . . She flew to the door. No, through the frosted glass she saw the welcome shape of Emma's sable, the broad outline of Roger behind. Her heart flowed with joy, with welcome as she threw open the door.

'Welcome . . .'

The smile stayed on her face despite the expression on the faces of Roger and Emma. Emma looked as if she had been crying and Roger was a curious pasty white as though he had been sick on the plane. Her heart turned to ice though she knew the smile remained. She must smile. She must.

'Harry?' she enquired, looking beyond them to where Harry would be getting the things out of the car. But the car was in darkness, the doors closed and there was no Harry. She looked at them. Harry was dead. She just stood silently to one side as they came past her, slowly into the sitting room.

That feeling of joy all day had been unnatural. Harry was dead.

3

Roger was a man who grew voluble on the subjects of wine, women and soccer; but when it came to explaining the nuances of deep personal relationships his verbal skills failed him. It was thus left to Emma to tell Alex that Harry had stayed behind at Beaune.

'Beaune?' Alex said, relief that Harry was alive not quite taking the place of the amazement she felt. 'Harry stayed on in Beaune?'

But if that was all, why the grim faces, the smudge of tears on Emma's cheeks? Harry bought wine in Beaune; it was quite a sensible place for him to be; but he might have warned her, sent word to avoid this awful disappointment. Even Alex the good wife, used to deferring to her partner in everything, felt let down by this.

'Harry stayed in Beaune . . .' Roger began and then his voice dried up. 'I could use a drink.'

Alex went to the drinks table and poured Roger a whisky without asking him what he wanted, which was a measure of her unease. She still had the feeling of dread, of not understanding. Yet Harry was alive.

'How peculiar of him not to let me know,' she said, her voice dull now with disappointment – about the meat, the wine, making love. What a hell of an anti-climax. She passed Roger his glass and then poured one for herself.

'Emma?'

'I'll stick to gin thanks, darling.'

'I suppose something cropped up at the last moment. But he could have rung me.'

She realized she was saying things very mechanically and they were trying so hard not to be ill at ease. Why? Then Roger sat down heavily on a chair and Emma stood in a rather dramatic pose. The green suit was terribly unbecoming with Emma looking so pale. Why did Emma look so pale, and Roger – why was he so nervous?

'Is there something you're not telling me?' Alex said, aware that her voice was rising. 'There is, isn't there? Is Harry ill?'

No answer.

'Roger this is ridiculous!' Alex burst out. 'What are you trying to do to me? What is the matter?'

'Well I suppose Harry *is* kind of ill,' Roger said puffing out his heavy moustache. 'At least I think he is.'

His words seemed to galvanize Emma, who moved quickly over to Alex. She tried to take her hand, but Alex kept them both firmly clasped in front of her, her figure upright.

'We think Harry's had some sort of breakdown, darling. Please sit down and try and relax. He's really quite all right . . .'

'Is he in hospital?'

'No no. It's not that sort of breakdown. Sort of emotional really. *Please* sit down, Alex.'

Alex sat down on the sofa, her hands still clasped stiffly in front of her. She was aware that her heart was beating regularly and slowly but very loudly, so that surely they would both be able to hear it.

Roger shuffled about and finally looked at Alex, opening his mouth and pressing his lips against his teeth.

'I think Harry has been working too hard, or something.'

'You mean in the *last two weeks*?' Alex said shrilly. 'He has had a breakdown through overwork in *two weeks*? He was perfectly fit when he left here and Harry has never overworked ever since I've known him. I mean not *overworked*. He works hard but not to the point of breakdown. Besides . . .'

'Yes, darling?' said Emma gently as though encouraging a child.

'Harry would have told me if something was wrong, bothering him. He would have talked to me about it . . .'

Roger got up helping himself to a second large whisky.

'I think we should go Emma,' he said. 'I'm tired.'

'Oh ROGER.' Emma expostulated. 'What are you talking about? We can't leave like this.'

'There's the meal,' Alex said, aware now of a suspicion

forming itself slowly in her mind, uncoiling like a long thin serpent. 'We should eat.'

She was not hungry and was aware the others were not either. Then she knew.

'Harry didn't *want* to come home?'

Emma nodded and Roger gasped and gazed earnestly at the ceiling, his teeth still sucking at his lips.

'Harry didn't want to come home,' Alex repeated flatly without the inflecton of enquiry at the end.

'Harry has a woman,' Emma said.

'Oh Emma!' Roger burst out.

'Well, that's what we've been trying to say, isn't it? We can't just leave her without telling her, Roger.'

Her voice rose as it always did when she was talking to Roger as though they were forever on the point of a ferocious argument.

'Harry has a woman,' Alex repeated, again like someone learning the lines for a play. She shook her shoulders and let her hands uncoil themselves and relax. 'You mean Harry is in Beaune with another woman?'

Emma nodded. Roger sighed.

Alex looked fixedly at Roger. It was Roger who should have been in Beaune with another woman. Not Harry. *Harry?* She got up and Emma quickly got up with her.

'Oh darling, don't break down. It won't last. Neither of us think it will last, do we Roger?'

Roger shook his head, but it could have meant yes or no.

'A Frenchwoman. Someone he just met?'

Roger shook his head again, but this time it seemed to mean no. Emma went and got another drink; taking a long time to splash tonic into her gin.

'Rosalind Vaughan,' Emma said with a note of rising indignation in her voice.

'Rosalind Vaughan?'

'She came to Beaune with us,' Roger said as though that satisfactorily explained the whole thing.

'It's been going on for some time,' Emma said. 'You might as well know.'

'Rosalind and *Harry*...'

Emma nodded, pursing her mouth.

'At least a year . . .'

'Harry and Rosalind have been having an affair for a year . . .'

'At least,' Roger said.

Alex sat down again.

'Why didn't anyone tell me?'

'People don't say these things, darling,' Emma said sitting next to her, very close and protecting. 'Especially to you. You were so happy.'

'I don't believe it,' Alex said at last. 'It couldn't be.' Of course it couldn't be with Harry; he and she knew each other like open books. This was Emma being bitchy again.

'It's absolutely true I'm afraid,' Roger said gathering courage from his wife. 'About a year. We never thought it would last.'

'You just said that. But it's already lasted a year. Harry and I met and got married within a year. It's a long time, a year. And now he's stayed on with her and not come home. It's incredible.'

'It is. Quite incredible,' Roger agreed relieved now that Alex was calming down. She really was a cold fish.

Alex was trying confusedly to conjure up a picture of Rosalind Vaughan who had been Roger's and Harry's secretary for about two years, just as she had been years ago at the wine merchants where she met Harry. Rosalind was a few years older than she had been then.

She wasn't anything special to look at – in Alex's opinion – tall, but otherwise nondescript. She'd been to the house once or twice for parties. She frequently talked with Alex on the phone, taking a message or explaining an absence of Harry's from the office. Alex had never really registered Rosalind Vaughan at all as anyone in particular. Yet Rosalind was Harry's girlfriend. She was the reason he hadn't come home after two weeks in France. Rosalind Vaughan.

Emma was watching Alex with an exaggerated awareness as if she expected that any moment she would do something quite untypical and extraordinary.

But Alex wasn't going to do anything like that. She was going to try and sort this thing out. Awful and incredible, but it could be sorted out. She and Harry were too rational, too unemotional to let their lives be muddied by something so untidy, as illogical as this.

'Did he send a message?' she said at last.

'Harry feels awful about this,' Roger said, gesticulating.

'I should think so,' said Emma. 'He should at least have come home and done the proper thing. Not left it to us. I shall never forgive Harry. Never.'

'It was a failure of nerve,' Roger said, beginning to stand up for his partner. 'Rosalind made a scene, said she was tired of the secrecy, the lying and so on. She absolutely refused to budge and Harry said he'd stay with her to sort it out. Had to. Said it was time you knew anyway.'

'But he gave you *no* message, no letter?'

Roger ran his fingers through his hair. 'It was all very much a last minute thing. We were all packed to come. It only happened today, Christ almighty! Harry came into my room rather upset and said Ros had wept all night and refused to get up . . .'

Now Alex blenched and shut her eyes. Harry and Rosalind in bed all night, every night for two weeks. Her strange body with Harry's familiar one, close together. It was this realization, this physical sharing of something she had thought belonged exclusively to her, that was going to be the most difficult thing to accept.

'Well we had discussions, what have you,' Roger continued. 'Harry was in a state, Ros was in a state. They got me into a state I can tell you. I said couldn't we get it all sorted out in London? Be all civilized and at least decent to Alex? Rosalind said that once they got home nothing would change. She knew Harry. They'd just go back to things as they were and she was sick of it. Harry had to make up his mind. You or her.'

'And he chose her, just like that?' Alex said faintly, thinking back on twelve years of happy marriage.

'No, no of course not, darling,' Emma looked crossly at Roger. 'She got at him, don't you see? Cunning little bitch. Two honeymoon weeks in beautiful France, plastered out of their minds every night . . . She got at him. Didn't she, Rog? *Rog,* I said didn't she get at him?'

'Yes,' Roger said angrily. 'I suppose she did.'

'It's so unlike Harry,' Alex said looking distractedly at the patio dining room, the low lights still on, the silver winking invitingly, the lace table cloth, the crisp linen table napkins . . .

'My God the beef . . . oh to hell with the beef,' Alex paused in the middle of diving for the kitchen. 'Is anyone hungry?'

'I could use a sandwich,' Roger said helping himself to more whisky.

'Trust you,' Emma looked at him contemptuously.

'What do you mean, trust me?'

'I mean in an hour of deep personal crisis all you think of is your bloody stomach . . .'

'Emma, that's not true. That is not true. I have a rotten job to do. Tell Alex her husband has left her . . .'

'Harry has not *left* her, you thoughtless beast,' Emma screamed. 'He just hasn't come home. It's not the same thing at all.'

'Maybe it is,' Alex said quietly. 'Maybe Roger knows that Harry is never coming home. Do you, Roger?'

'No, I do not. The whole thing only blew up today as I told you. It was a complete surprise, a shock to me. I knew about Ros, the bloody thing has been going on under my nose for over a year, but this is the first time Harry ever went away with her for so long . . .'

'But he did go away before?' Alex still felt rather detached from the whole thing, as though she were one of those women lawyers you saw on the telly being very crisp and clever in court. 'Harry has been away with her before?'

'Well you know the odd trip. There was Alsace in the spring, Bordeaux a few weeks ago . . .'

Every trip Harry always said how sorry he was she couldn't come; he always had. She remembered particularly his saying it even this time. 'I wish you were coming, darling!' Yet he had known as he said it that he was going with his secretary.

'Look,' Roger said, 'I really am tired. I do want to go home and sleep. Let's talk tomorrow. I've had enough of this cross-examination. It's not as though it was my fault . . .'

'Roger! I think you owe it to Alex at least to try and explain things to her; help her. You can't just leave her, Roger.'

'Well what the hell can I do?' Roger glanced wildly at the clock. 'I can't stay here all night! It's nearly midnight.'

Alex thought idly that she was glad she hadn't lit the candles.

They would have burnt out by now. She glanced again at the table as though it was a silent testimony to what might have been, should have been. The picture of the dining room on this night, like the happiness of the day that preceded it and the burning leaves in the park would remain forever etched on her mind, she was sure.

In the foreground she was conscious that Emma and Roger were engaged in one of their full-scale rows. 'Selfish', 'brute', 'thoughtless' were being hurled at Roger who was countering with 'spiteful', 'cat', and she even thought she heard 'whore' at one time, but surely it couldn't have been that. Alex vaguely wished they'd both go, was still wishing it when Roger rushed past her and she heard the front door bang violently. Then the car outside started up and when she became aware of things again Emma was lighting about her fiftieth cigarette that day and trembling.

'Pig!'

'Emma what are you doing here? Why didn't you go with Roger?'

'Him? You think I want to go with *him*? The thoughtless, selfish, stinking, male chauvinistic . . .'

'Oh Emma,' Alex laughed for the first time that evening and put her hand on Emma's arm. 'Roger did have a very hard job. I think he did the best he could.'

'He could have done more, been more of a support. Darling, I'm staying the night with you. No I insist. I'll sleep in the guest room. I want to be with you and near you and help in the morning. I'll take the girls to school.'

Suddenly Alex felt weak and child-like. She wanted now to cry. Emma was being such a brick, such a real friend . . . She sank down on the sofa and Emma sat next to her.

'Give in. Come on. Have a good cry.'

Alex looked in front of her up at the clock which said it was just midnight. The day, or rather yesterday, seemed to have been dominated by the clock. Waiting for Harry . . . the longing . . . the anticipation . . .

'Do you think he'll ever come home again?' she said frowning at the clock. 'Or has he gone forever?'

Emma gave a deep throaty sigh and coughed her smoker's rasp.

'I don't know, darling. I really don't know. Come on let me see you up to bed.'

'What about the beef?'

'To hell with the beef. You go right upstairs and I'll just switch everything off and make us some tea. Like some tea?'

'Mmmm . . .'

* * *

Later Alex sat propped up in bed while Emma walked about the room undressing. She'd refused the tranquillizer Emma had offered from her bag respite her reassurances that they didn't have any nasty effect. Alex had never taken a sedative in her life and only sleeping pills when they forced them on to her in the maternity hospital.

She'd turned back the bed when she'd dressed, leaving just the two bedside lights on and Harry's pyjamas at one side and her cool white linen nightie at the other. Now she was in the nightie between the turned-back sheets and Harry's pyjamas had been unemotionally put back in his drawer and his bedside lamp switched off.

Alex had kept firmly to her side, however, as she did when he was away, as though saving the other half for him. She sipped the tea Emma had poured.

'It will all be different tomorrow,' Emma said, as she wandered about in various stages of undress, dropping things on the floor and putting her jewellery on the dressing-table.

'There darling,' Emma stretched on the bed beside Alex and took her tea from Harry's bedside table. Emma was looking at her feet – brown and straight and rather big, wiggling her toes.

'You're very good, Emma, to stay.' Alex turned to her. 'It will help with the kids tomorrow.'

Emma gave her a brilliant smile, her blue eyes and clear white teeth glinting in the dull light.

'That's what friends are for, sweetheart. I'll stay as long as you like.'

'Oh no! I'll be perfectly all right. Besides there's Roger and Portia . . .'

'Portia can stay on here; she'd like nothing better. Roger can go to hell. He's probably dying to get into the arms of the latest popsie. Probably there now. Let's ring . . .'

Impulsively Emma put a hand out towards the phone, her

arm brushing across Alex as she did. Alex was aware of the arm against her own full breasts, thinly protected by her nightie. She shrank back to avoid the contact.

'Oh Emma, you're not going to ring home?'

'Why not? I'm curious anyway.'

Emma crouched over Alex who saw that she actually had a look of excitement in her eyes as she dialled. Did she really want Roger not to be there?

The phone rang and then Roger's gruff tired voice answered. Like a naughty little girl Emma replaced the receiver with a delighted smile.

'But why didn't you say it was you?'

'Let him think what he likes.'

Emma put the phone back, brushing again past Alex and leaned back on the pillow her arms behind her head.

'It's ridiculous, isn't it? It should be the other way round.'

'You mean Roger?'

'I've always been expecting him to go off. Just not come back one night, like . . .' her voice faltered.

'Like tonight?' Alex prompted.

'Yes. I never thought it would be Harry.'

'But you should have known that if Harry was having an affair it would be more serious.'

'I never thought of it that way. I thought men were all the same.'

'You *expect* them to be unfaithful?'

Emma looked at her with some surprise.

'Yes. In a way I suppose I do.'

'And you thought Harry was clever deceiving me and carrying on with his secretary?'

'Yes, if you like. I didn't think *this* would happen of course, not in a million years.'

'And you never told me because it was your sort of code of honour? Your own peculiar honour?'

'I suppose so.'

'I think you're corrupt, Emma.'

'Darling!' Emma looked at her with astonishment. 'Is that a nice thing to say?'

'Not very.' Alex realized she now felt bitter, but against Emma not against Harry. 'But I think it is a form of corruption to pretend to be a close friend and not even warn me Harry was having an affair. I think it's . . . unclean.'

For a while Emma was silent, sipping her tea and looking at the mirror at the end of the bed in which both women could see themselves.

'You're very innocent Alex. I'm not even going to be angry at what you say. I pity you for being so naïve.'

'And I pity you for being so cynical.'

'But I'm right, aren't I? Aren't I right to be cynical? Look at Harry. Why did Harry have to wander? Didn't he have everything he wanted? Here? Didn't he have a pretty wife, two attractive intelligent children, a lovely house beautifully kept, an excellent table and cellar. Didn't he have all that? The only thing I can think of that would make Harry wander is sex.'

'Sex?'

'Your sex life. You'd never talk about it.'

'I never talked about it because I never needed to. I didn't need either to boast about it or be comforted. It was good. Very good.'

Emma's eyes glittered with interest. She put her head on one side and nodded. Of course good for some people wasn't good enough for others. Somehow Alex hadn't satisfied Harry, that was obvious. But she couldn't say so. Instead she said softly:

'Then he *is* a sod.'

Now the tears did well up. Alex tried to choke them back but without success. They seemed to come from a great depth and leapt up through her throat, out of her eyes, her mouth. She blubbered and she spluttered, wept without control.

Finally, after a long time, she was quiet, aware of Emma's cool hand on her bare shoulder, patting her gently as though she were a baby.

'There, there,' Emma crooned, 'there, there.'

Then, thinking Alex was asleep, Emma switched off the bedside lights and crept out of the room, leaving the door ajar.

But Alex continued to lie on her stomach, her cheek pressed to the pillow, her fingers plucking at the under sheet, her eyes wide open, listening to that unnaturally loud beating of her heart.

4

The most difficult thing for Alex during the week that followed was trying to keep up appearances. Not only to appear, but to endeavour to feel, normal. She had no experience of a fundamental disturbance to the rhythm of life such as this, though one read about it all the time – deaths, accidents, people disappeared, fathers, and mothers apparently, suddenly left home. But to the *Twentymans*? One day you were in the mainstream of society and the next you were outside it.

The children knew there was something unusual about Harry's not coming home, something insufficiently explained. There was the appearance of their mother, pale and nervous however composed she tried to be, smoking a lot; and the flapping about of Aunt Emma who had even stayed the night. Alex told them that Daddy unexpectedly had to stay in France. For how long? She didn't know. She packed them off to school and collected them again, washed clothes and made the beds on the days she had no help, shopped, and even did a little gardening – but mentally she was somewhere in France with Harry. But where?

The worst thing, the really incredible thing, was not hearing from Harry. Not a line, or a word on the phone or the slightest gesture through a third person like Roger. Could you actually go off and do this sort of thing? Apparently you could. People did; now that you mentioned it Emma knew, or rather knew of, ever so many. But of course Harry was the *last* person . . .

It didn't help. Nothing helped. And the thing was that, tangibly at any rate, her world could function perfectly well without Harry. There was no problem with money because they had a joint bank account. Alex, the perfect housekeeper, always paid the bills anyway, rang the gas, electricity, called the plumber. In fact from her new perspective she saw with some surprise that there was very little contribution Harry actually made to the running order of the Twentyman household apart from being father, husband, and its titular head. Alex had never been one to say 'Harry could you fetch this or bring that? Go here or go there.' Never. Practically all Harry saw to was the running of his business and both their cars – cars being so much a male preserve – otherwise he just had to eat, sleep and exist in perfect comfort.

But it was the emotional presence of Harry that was lacking; that was missed. To know that Harry was coming home at night, leaving in the morning; that he was there, that it was his place. His drawers, his cupboard, his dressing-gown, his towel, his place at table. Without Harry the household was incomplete; it was as simple as that.

In a way it was as though Harry had died, that the plane had crashed and he was no more. In many ways, Alex thought in her bitter moments, of which there were many, it might have been better.

But it wasn't so much rage that Alex felt against Harry as total incomprehension. How could someone behave so atypically? What went on in a person's mind when they did this? How could you grasp it? Of all the people in the world abruptly to desert wife and family, Harry Twentyman was about the last one you would have thought of, everyone agreed about that. Because of course the fact was that, largely thanks to Emma Drax, everyone pretty soon did know about it.

Emma was genuinely so horrified about the whole thing that she couldn't help letting it out. At first she told the Reverend Mother at the convent for fear that Alex, who had always so depended upon Harry, would have a complete nervous breakdown. Then when she saw how quickly Alex recovered, how soon she was able to cope, she was so full of admiration she couldn't resist holding her up as a spectacle of magnificent liberated womanhood. ('You wouldn't think to look at her, would you . . .?')

Alex was aware of this the day, exactly a week after Harry's non-arrival (you couldn't call it a disappearance) when Rachel emerged alone from the school, flung herself into the car and gave vent to a torrent of weeping.

'Darling, whatever is the matter?'

Nothing came from Rachel except great sniffles, snuffles and floods and floods of tears. Alex got into the back seat and took the weeping child into her arms.

'There, darling, tell me what it is. Did you quarrel with someone?'

Sniffle, sniffle.

'What is it, Rachel? I cannot help you if I don't know.'

Rachel suddenly looked out of the car window and began her commotion anew.

'See they all know; they're looking at us!'

Alex looked distractedly out of the window. True a few faces did look towards her car with interest, but who wouldn't be curious at the spectacle that was presented therein? Then she knew; because the mothers, their faces carefully averted, were hurrying the children past the car, telling them not to look. The mothers knew of course, and so did the children. Alex got into the front seat and drove quickly off.

By the time they got home Rachel was quieter, but when she saw Toby on the doorstep she burst into tears all over again. Toby, whose sister's moods were a source of indifference to him, looked bored and chewed at an apple.

'Hi Mum,' he opened the door and bent in to kiss her, jerking his head in the direction of the back seat.

'Hello, darling. Sorry we're late. Can you get my shopping out of the boot?'

She gave him the keys and took Rachel carefully by the shoulders easing her out and making soothing noises as she led her into the house, Toby following.

'Daddy's not coming back!' Rachel bawled dramatically as soon as the door was shut. 'He has left home!' And she flung herself at the chest of her brother who staggered uncertainly under her weight and looked at his mother.

Alex didn't know what to say. She took off Rachel's coat and sat her on her knees, smoothing back her thick dark hair, the strands on the forehead wet from weeping.

'Who told you that?'

'P . . . Portia. She heard her mummy and daddy talking about it. She says her mummy talks of nothing else she's so upset. She asked P . . . Portia to say n . . . nothing . . .'

Rachel leaned on her mother's chest and began sucking her thumb, the tears less dramatic now. Alex continued to stroke her head and look over it at Toby who was studying the core of his apple.

'Is it true, Mum?'

'I don't know.' Alex considered her small son who, though just 10, was such a support, such a companion. Was he going to have to be the man of the house from now on? Old before his time?

'What do you mean you don't *know*?'

'It's true Daddy was expected back from France and didn't come.'

'Why?'

'He hasn't told me.'

'What do you mean he hasn't told you?'

'Don't be rude, Toby, don't repeat every word I say.'

Alex was irritated by his accusing tones, his rough aggressive voice, though she understood the reason for it. This was Toby's way of expressing shock. Besides, he adored his father. She put an arm out and drew him to her, kissing his cheek.

'Daddy just decided not to come back with Roger. He didn't tell me why and he hasn't sent a message or anything.'

'You mean you haven't heard from Dad at all?'

'No.'

'Perhaps he's ill.'

'No he's not ill, that I do know.'

'Is it something we've done? You've done, Mum? Did you have a row?'

'No nothing. Or maybe it is something I've done, but over a long period.'

'How do you mean?'

'Well maybe Daddy wasn't very happy with me, not as happy as I was with him, and I didn't know it.'

'But Daddy was happy with you, Mum, and us. He was always kissing you.'

Alex shut her eyes; the memory of Harry's affection tormenting her again. The casual smack on the lips, the touch on the nape of the neck, the tongue deeply in the mouth with passion. Yes Harry was always kissing her – perhaps he was always kissing Rosalind too. Habits like that were hard to drop.

The vision of Rosalind helped her a lot and she held back the tears in her throat and shrugged.

'I don't understand what's happened and Daddy hasn't told me. Now maybe he'll just walk in that door and all will be well, or maybe he won't. If he won't talk to me or tell me, I can't predict what's going to happen.'

Alex took the quietened Rachel off her knee and filled the kettle. She lit a cigarette and leaned against one of the many shiny working surfaces of their expensively built-in kitchen.

'It's not like Dad.' Toby said beginning to show his wounded feelings. 'You wouldn't have thought Dad would do a thing like that.' He looked at his mother as though a reason had occurred to him too – the nuclear-age child who knew all about adult relationships from even a quite minimal exposure to television. 'Unless he's got someone else? Doesn't he like us any more?'

Rachel used that opportunity to have another fit of outraged sobbing and Alex this time did feel like joining her. It was wearing her down – and it was Friday and she'd have the weekend to get through, just her and the children. They'd all be shut in the house in a cocoon of grief.

Alex blinked back the tears and busied herself with the teapot.

'*Has* he got someone else, Mum?'

She felt Toby close up to her, pressing against her, his gruff anxious voice appealing to her to reassure him. But she couldn't.

'I don't know, darling, I really don't know anything until I speak to Daddy.'

'But can't you go and see him? Don't you know where he is?'

No, that she wouldn't do. She'd thought of it; getting on a plane and raging over to wherever Harry was. But where was he? Roger seemed to think the lovers had planned to go south to Italy or the Riviera. Roger was already angry that Harry had taken this time off not only from his family but also from the business. Roger hadn't heard from Harry either, or rather he said that he hadn't. And, Roger had added tactlessly, they hadn't even got a secretary either.

That week Emma Drax had flitted in and out constantly,

whispering to Alex, feeding her comforting titbits when the children had gone to bed. It was very sweet of Emma, and Alex knew she only meant well. But she had proved to be a treacherous friend; and if accused she would deny it indignantly.

As if choosing the exact moment to appear, Emma rushed through the back door dragging Portia also bawling and looking fatter than ever. Emma thrust Portia into the middle of the room and began to administer to her chubby arms a succession of slaps that, in Alex's opinion, didn't improve the atmosphere in the kitchen one little bit because Rachel started to howl again and Toby went an angry red and stamped out of the room.

'She's a naughty . . . (slap) . . . stupid . . . (slap) . . . wicked . . . (slap) . . . girl . . .'

'Oh Emma, please!' Alex kneaded the palms of her hands to her ears as though trying to block out the sounds of weeping, wailing and slapping. Emma was red-faced too, her bright blue eyes lit up with hatred, her teeth bared in a snarl. Her pretty short fair curly hair seemed to Alex to flare up about her head now like the halo of an avenging angel.

'I'm *so* sorry, Alex.'

'What's done is done.' The sort of philosophical thing people would expect Alex to say she said, with a shrug of the shoulders. 'Harry could just walk in that door any moment and then a lot of trouble, a lot of gossip would have been caused for nothing.'

Emma looked at her with withering pity, Emma having heard that day from Roger that the lovers were not only in St Remo but having a wonderful time. A postcard if you please! Roger had gone to a lot of trouble reading the postcard and describing the picture on it to Emma, his voice betraying a gritty quality, an indication of what he would like to do to Harry when he saw him. Harry's defection had brought Roger and Emma closer together. They now had something to talk about, something in common and consequently talked about nothing else. They couldn't wait to see each other to discuss this business of Harry and Rosalind Vaughan all over again.

Eventually Alex persuaded the girls to stop crying and ordered them up to the playroom with Toby on the promise of a large beefburger tea in half an hour. She got the minced beefburger meat out of the fridge and began mixing it in a bowl with finely chopped onion, water and an egg. She did it with her hands so that she got a better consistency. Emma sat and watched her, smoking and drinking cold tea. She thought that Alex looked pale; but that could have been her period or a tiring day, not the sort of weariness that a woman whose husband had just deserted her, *deserted* her, ought to show. Maybe, as Emma had always thought (what woman, after all, *didn't* like talking about sex?), Alex was too cold and maybe that was why Harry had preferred the sophisticated charms of Rosalind Vaughan. Maybe Rosalind was hot stuff in bed.

For Rosalind was sophisticated, both Emma and Roger agreed on that. She was cool and calculating and you could sense that all along she had known what she was doing, planned this operation to coincide with the annual visit to Burgundy. The odd thing was that Rosalind was not unlike Alex in looks, tall and fair (well mousy hair really, but fairish) and with an air of assurance that irritated smaller less good-looking women like, well, Emma for instance. Only the difference was that whereas Alex radiated happiness which seemed to come from her love for Harry and the children, her delight in her home and her way of life, just the sort of life she'd planned and wanted, Rosalind habitually wore a bored rather discontented look on her face that accentuated her pert upturned nose and the sculptural curves of her sensual mouth.

Emma knew that Roger of course had had a good crack at Rosalind first and had had to retire in disorder, not quite unmanned (he said) but admitting defeat. It was Rosalind who had made a play for Harry, not the other way round. Rosalind's seduction of Harry had been part of a long strategic battle manoeuvre which was to attain final victory in the vineyards of Burgundy.

'I'd like to get in touch with Harry,' Alex said in her calm voice, kneading the beefburgers before rolling them into balls, and covering them with flour. 'For the children's sakes as well as mine, of course. He must be in touch with Roger.'

'He's not,' Emma said making a face at the last dregs of the cold tea. 'Roger is very angry about it. It's having a bad effect on the business. Things are hard enough as it is. I think Roger thinks Harry has gone off his head,' and she told Alex about the postcard.

'Imagine a length of sandy beach covered with half naked brown bodies. "Having a wonderful time, wish you were here," kind of thing. Harry has to countersign cheques, you know, approve deals . . . '

'Roger should have thought of that when he left him in Beaune . . .'

'Darling, what could Rog think? He was flabbergasted, all packed up and the car leaving for Lyons airport in an hour, that sort of thing. He imagined Harry would sort it all out with Rosalind and fly home almost at once.'

Alex nodded.

'Yes, that would be the reasonable thing to do. Do you know legally there's not a thing I can do about Harry, at the moment. He's not a missing person, he doesn't owe us money. He's just gone off, and I have to wait until he comes back. Anyway, Harry has to be in touch with Roger soon about the business. Would you ask Roger to pass the message that I need to talk to him quite quietly and without fuss and that I must see him.'

'Of course, darling,' Emma came up to her and pressed her arm, that contact again, that powerful scent of Emma's that Alex associated with terribly expensive fur salons. She moved away and dropped the beefburgers into the bubbling fat.

'Alex, I'm so sorry . . .'

'About what?'

'About Portia telling . . . it's just been so awfully hard, the shock, to keep it to ourselves . . . I never dreamed she'd hear.'

Alex shrugged, shaking the heavy skillet. 'Maybe it's best it all came out after all, and if Harry is sending picture postcards from Italy who knows where from next. Maybe Greece?' She turned round and smiled at Emma, a smile of almost pure amusement, Emma thought, extraordinary girl. 'Maybe he is going to be like that man who went all round the world leaving a trail and a sorrowing wife behind him. Call the kids, would you?'

Emma shook her head and went to the stairs. There was a lot about Alex not only that she didn't know, but that she didn't understand. She was a curious person for someone like Emma, with her warm impulsive nature, to have for a friend.

* * *

The weeks of October went by and early November came and Alex thought how odd it was that they began to live with, and accept, an abnormal situation as something normal. Despite knowing what she knew she tried to regard it as an extension of Harry's business trip or to pretend, say, that he had a long period in hospital or that she was the wife of an arctic explorer.

But what she had to accustom herself to, what was so strange to her after twelve years, was what the wives of explorers did about sex when their husbands were marooned in the antarctic for months, years maybe, on end. The first thing she found was that it didn't bother her, she didn't think about it; and then that she gradually did, that she thought about it and wanted it, and dreamed about it, especially knowing that Harry was on a sort of honeymoon with a pretty and younger girl and was doubtless having it quite often.

As with everything else – running the house, dealing with people's embarrassed enquiries, keeping the children occupied – Alex tried to deal with the sex problem as she did with the rest of her life, by not dwelling on it, keeping herself occupied, under control.

But for how long? The explorer husband eventually came home, even after two years. For all she knew Harry never would or, if he did, it would be to get his things, not to go to bed with her. And in twelve years Alex Twentyman had never been the slightest bit attracted by any other man. She had never had an affair, never even flirted, or at least not consciously flirted, with the object of actually entrapping a man as Emma did all the time, only her efforts had the opposite effect. Or did Emma really want another man? Didn't she just want to make Roger jealous, show him she could wander too?

Alex found she began to resent all those wives who went to bed with their husbands every night. She had it on her mind, and she'd look at people in the street and wonder when they'd last had sex. The night before? That morning? Were they hurrying off to a lunch-time assignation in some trendy flat in Swiss Cottage or Belsize Park after a delicious little lunch at a Greek restaurant in Camden Town? Who knew? Why was it so important anyway?

And so the days passed, the autumn colours changed, the branches of the trees in the park were finally bare or nearly so, and Roger was at his wits' end when Harry Twentyman came back to London and took up residence with his girlfriend Rosalind Vaughan in her flat off the Earl's Court Road.

5

Harry had been away a month, when he came back, almost to the day he was supposed to return. Apparently he ran out of money and Roger refused to send him any, or the banks on the continent to advance him any more on the strength of his credit cards. Rosalind didn't have any money; anyway she didn't think it a woman's place to pay, even if she had. She was quite sure about that sort of thing – she was all for equality, fair play between the sexes, mutual enjoyment in bed, but not for women forking out when they were accompanied by men.

Alex heard that Harry had returned when she came back from taking Rachel to school and she was exhausted by the sympathetic conversations that so many well-meaning mothers tried to engage her in, offering their support, anything they could do, a month was a long time, wasn't it, did she know a good lawyer? Already there was an air of apartness Alex felt about herself and Rachel, and she now refused a good many invitations to tea so that she wouldn't have to go through those inquisitive prodding talks over sherry in the drawing room, or reciprocate by inviting anyone back.

For Alex was beginning to wilt. All that uncertainty, all that control, all that stiff-upper-lip and trying to be normal had a debilitating effect. From being very fit and well she had gradually become rather run-down and tired, little spots appeared on her face, her back hurt and her period came two weeks early instead of being regularly on the dot every twenty-eight days.

Emma said she was carrying too big a burden but what could she do about it? Emma recommended her analyst, Dr Dickson, but Alex couldn't face the prospect despite the wonders he had allegedly worked for Emma. Harry's parents were dead and hers lived in Scotland. She hadn't even told her mother about Harry and didn't want to until she had to. Mrs Buchanan was frail enough without hearing that her idolized son-in-law was making her daughter unhappy. Alex's brother Alistair was a mining engineer in South America and they only corresponded at Christmas time and saw each other every five years. Alex had no sisters and, she realized, no really close friends.

She had given twelve years of her life exclusively to Harry – no that wasn't fair – she had *shared* twelve years of her life with Harry, shared friends, shared activities. Harry was her husband and her lover and her best friend. Harry was her world and that world now was empty except for people like Emma and a few other women who were mostly the mothers of friends of Rachel and Toby, or people she met casually. They were peripheral friends whose real lives, like hers used to, centred on their husbands and their children, their well-kept homes and gardens and their other circle of friends whom they only knew in this domestic context.

Alex had read a number of novels on this subject and seen a good many plays about it on the TV; but she had actually never lived through it herself. She was beginning to realize what an isolating and chilling experience it was. And it was only just beginning. From this point she could see no end to it unless a miracle happened and Harry repented of his behaviour and came home.

And if he did what would she do? Would she want him? Yes.

* * *

'Harry suggests you meet for lunch,' Roger said on the phone, his voice casual because he was embarrassed and also resented this role into which he had been cast. Indignation rose in Alex's throat.

'Oh did he? And I have to cry all over Luigi's or whatever.'

'I don't think Harry imagines you will break down,' Roger's strained almost unfriendly voice continued. 'Harry says you've always got so much control. He thinks it will be more civilized that way.'

What Harry means, Alex thought, is that I won't be able to make a scene or appeal to his heart strings or his better nature by showing him his own familiar home.

'Harry suggested Luigi's actually,' Roger went on. 'He says you are both known there. Tomorrow at one if that's all right.'

Tomorrow at one. A date with her husband. As she put the phone down Alex found that she was trembling, and crying and losing control. Her heart was pounding and she felt a hysteria she had never experienced in her life before. A world carefully built up that was falling to pieces. She had no religious faith, no support and no pills, nothing to hang on to and nowhere to go.

Yet after she went to fetch Rachel, and Toby came home she took them across the road into the park in the dusk and walked around taking deep breaths as they played on the swings. They seemed particularly happy that day shouting and laughing and she kneaded her fists in her pockets and knew that, for them, she must make the effort, she must regain control. If the past month had been anything to go by, Harry would provide little emotional support for them for a while, at least. Maybe forever.

* * *

Luigi's was in Soho, a small Italian restaurant that she and Harry had been to several times a year since they were first married. It was comfortable, and rather dark and anyway familiar so that if she cried it wouldn't be in a strange fearful place. She was glad he'd chosen Luigi's.

She hadn't told the children he was home or that she was meeting him. She'd had to endure Emma for almost an hour – or so it seemed, though it was probably less – on the phone that morning telling Alex what she would tell Harry were she Alex. She would tell him this that and the other, oh yes where to get off AND she'd mention the business because if Harry thought that Roger . . .

On it went, but it did pass the time and Alex found it otherwise a very long morning in which to dress carefully and prepare herself for meeting her own husband who, in four weeks, had become a stranger.

She purposely didn't wear anything that Harry especially liked. She purposely didn't make herself up too much or try in any way to look sexy. She wanted to be herself – no ploys, no subterfuge. Just Alex.

Harry was in the restaurant when she got there. She'd tried to imagine what it would be like to see him again, and when she did she got a shock and a thrill, just like being in love. Knowing that she still was in love with him; that he still excited her, that she found him attractive. How he moved and looked, the clothes he wore, his airs and manners, the distinct smell of Harry when you got close to him – a nice earthy fresh smell, manly and wholesome.

Harry stood up awkwardly when he saw Alex. He was a big man and it was a small table so that he nearly pushed it over and the diversion made Luigi himself run up and greet Mrs Twentyman and ask how she was, and the children? Then smiling he put her tenderly next to Harry and gently pushed the table back again. She wished she'd sat opposite Harry and not next to him. His presence was too familiar to her. When they sat here usually it was after a play or a cinema and their thighs would touch and their legs in the close confined space, or their shoulders as they leaned together afterwards drinking a brandy and smoking and knowing that they'd make love when they got home. But Harry had moved along the upholstered bench that ran along the wall and was gazing at her with a very polite, pleasant and totally strange expression on his face as though this was someone to whom he had been unexpectedly introduced.

'Alex!'

He leaned over and kissed her cheek and she smelt that smell, that special Harry smell and felt his smoothly shaved face.

'And how are you, Alex?'

She looked at him aware that her eyes were hard and mocking.

'Oh fine,' she said, 'really fine.'

'Good, good . . .' Harry looked away from her at the tablecloth and started drawing patterns on it with his fork. He looked thoughtful, she saw. Was he taken in by her casualness? Was he taken in by himself?

Luigi came and they ordered antipasto and veal, a bottle of Verdicchio. Alex frankly thought that food would choke her, but she must contrive. She could always eat a little and leave the rest. When Luigi left there was a silence that neither she nor Harry tried to fill.

She took a grissono from the tall glass jar in the centre of the table and nibbled it.

'It's very awkward, Alex . . .'

She said nothing. Let him talk. He continued drawing frenzied patterns on the table cloth with his fork. He looked well. He was brown and had put on a bit of weight. Well, so he should. He had had all that sun, eaten a lot of food, drunk a great deal of wine no doubt and had plenty of sex. He should look well on it. She would have too.

'Alex . . .' He looked at her and moved closer as though drawn by her familiarity as she was to his. 'It's terribly difficult to know how to begin.'

'I should think it must be,' Alex said, aware her tone was detached and unfriendly.

'Oh Alex, don't be bitter, for God's sake. It can't help. Don't you see how difficult it was for me?'

'It wasn't easy for me either, the last month. Not knowing . . .'

A look of bewilderment came over Harry's face.

'But surely you knew?'

Alex stared in amazement at him, this husband of hers, a man she had been married to for twelve years, known thirteen.

'*Knew*? That you weren't coming home?'

'No . . . about Rosalind. She was sure you knew.'

'How did she think I knew?'

'By your voice, the way you looked at her. She thought she detected hostility. She thought you'd known for ages.'

'I hardly noticed her at all to tell you the truth,' Alex said as witheringly as she could in the circumstances. 'I wouldn't say she was one to stand out in a crowd.'

'Oh she's a good-looking girl,' Harry said defensively. 'Not as attractive as you of course . . .'

'Then *why*, Harry?'

Harry was silent, looking at some point in the restaurant to the left of Alex's shoulder.

'*Why*, Harry? You must answer me. I must know.'

'Well I can't explain it; not in words. It's not rational I

suppose. And then when I thought you knew and didn't mind, well I suppose I imagined I could just keep it like that. But Rosalind . . .'

'Didn't,' Alex finished for him. 'She'd had enough. Harry, knowing me – I suppose you do know me though God knows I thought I knew you – do you think I could have silently condoned an affair and said nothing?'

'Well, knowing you, Alex, I thought yes, that's what you would do. You'd take it calmly and keep control. You'd carry on as you were. You're so capable, Alex.'

'But, Harry, it's the *last* thing I'd do. Knowing me how could you possibly say that?'

She looked at him with amazement, with anger, with fear.

'Well maybe I didn't know you. Maybe I didn't know you, Alex, after all. Ah, food.'

Harry leaned back with a pleased grateful expression, as though he were so hungry he could eat a horse. His large hands were palms downwards on the table and the white cuffs of his shirt showed a couple of inches between his grey suit and dark brown, sunburnt hands. She looked at them with the long brown fingers, black tufts of hair, and evenly pared well kept nails. There was something very personal and intimate about hands – his hands had explored her body, every intimate inch of it many times. She had smelt her smells on his fingers as he licked them before dipping them into her again. She closed her eyes. And Rosalind too . . . the technique would be the same. Only the person was different.

She took up her fork and stuck it into a hard piece of tuna. It was quite dry and difficult to digest. She sipped from the glass of cool Verdicchio before putting her fork on the plate again. Harry was eating hungrily. Scoffing really.

'So you didn't know me, Harry?'

'No, perhaps not. I don't think we ever know one another do we really? I mean to be honest. I've done a lot of thinking, Alex, I really have, and basically I think everyone is alone.'

'How profound. Especially as you weren't at the time.'

'Don't be sarcastic, Alex, it won't help. Besides it isn't like you.'

'But you didn't know me. You just said so.'

Harry wiped the antipasto juice from the plate with his roll and licked his fingers in a gesture of immense satisfaction. He drained his glass of wine and poured some more.

'Well I've thought about it as I said. I don't think we knew each other. Couldn't have for this to happen.'

'What to happen, Harry?'

Harry gave an expansive gesture in the direction of the restaurant at large and shrugged.

'Well all this. Rosalind, me to go away, not come home. I never thought I'd do that did you?'

'No.'

'There. It shows we don't know each other . . . or *ourselves*, Alex,' he added profoundly, leaning towards her, his thin almost bloodless lips compressed. Then he took up a toothpick and inserted it in his mouth.

'Harry, what am I to understand? That you had an affair because you didn't know me or because you did and you wanted to get away?'

'It's not as simple as that Alex. Don't try and be so explicit, please. Oh thank you . . .' he leaned back again eagerly as the waiter put the veal scallopine before them. 'Alex, you aren't eating?' He looked surprised as Alex pushed her antipasto away and smiled up at the waiter; then he shrugged. This frequent shrugging was a new gesture to Alex. Undoubtedly the Gallic influence acquired after a month's immersion on the continent.

'Look, Alex; we've been married what, twelve years?'

'I thought we were close.'

Alex tried to keep that brittle tone in her voice, but it broke and she found she couldn't go on. Her eyes were filling with tears and she bent her head to her plate. Harry, as though recognizing the break in her voice, stopped eating and leaned towards her.

'Of *course*, darling, we're close.'

His voice was completely different; his brown eyes looked tenderly at her. He took his white handkerchief from his top pocket and dabbed at the corner of her eyes.

'There, darling, don't let go. Of course we're close.'

'Then what is it,' Alex spoke very slowly and brokenly, tears openly showing now, 'that you are trying to say?'

Harry took her hand and squeezed it, stroking the back with

his thumb.

'I don't know. I want you to help me.'

'How . . . how can *I* help you?'

She gave a big sniff and grabbed again at the glass.

'I want us to try and understand what all this is about. Just because I . . . well I've gone off . . . having an affair, whatever it is, with Rosalind doesn't mean you are nothing to me, Alex. How can we just forget the last twelve years?'

Alex felt she didn't want to cry any more; but she knew her eyes were moist and her nose probably pink. She wanted to be reasonable, above all just. But why was he trying to blame her? What part had she played? She'd just stayed at home and done what she thought was the right thing, being a good, loving wife.

'But I didn't try and break it Harry. I was very happy.'

'And I was happy too, I don't want you to think I wasn't. It's just . . .'

'You weren't happy enough?'

He looked at her shrewdly as though that was the word. Then he frowned.

'No . . . that's not what I mean. I was very happy; but . . .' He gazed at her almost pathetically, she thought, trying to harden her heart again. 'Well I fell in love with Rosalind. I fell in love again. I didn't mean to and I didn't want to. I couldn't help it. When I did . . . then I thought I wasn't as happy as I imagined I had been, if you understand me. I mean, because I could love *her,* I couldn't have been happy, could I? Not completely happy?'

Alex tried to think about it, but all she felt was confusion.

'When did you realize it was serious about Rosalind?' She kept her voice low and quiet, as would be expected of the perfect wife trying to be helpful and understanding.

'Oh, quite soon. But I still loved you, Alex, and I still *do.* That part of us is precious to me.'

Alex suddenly felt she was going to be sick. She smelt the tuna in her mouth and the veal almost choked her. Tears came to her eyes and she coughed. She patted her chest and took another deep draught of wine.

'Are you all right?'

'Yes,' she pushed the plate away. 'I don't think I can eat any more. I'm sorry, Harry. This conversation is completely beyond me, or above me, I don't know which. I don't understand at all why an apparently happily married man who is well looked after, affectionate to his children and who makes frequent love to his wife . . .' she said the words very slowly and looked at him sharply. 'I don't understand why this person falls in love with someone else.'

Harry was looking soulfully at the table shaking his head.

'Neither do I, Alex. I *did* desire you . . .'

'You made love to me and Rosalind at the same time. Well not the same time, you know what I mean . . .'

Harry nodded his head in full understanding, that expression of boyish bewilderment continuing to trouble his face. 'And you would have gone on like that, Harry, making love to us both, maybe on the same day, most probably on the same day come to think of it, well, forever?'

'Maybe.' Harry said quietly.

'But Rosalind put a stop to it?'

'Well . . .'

'She got you out of the country and she said "I'm not going back until you promise to leave your wife. I can't stand this any more." '

Once more Harry nodded eagerly, his expression grateful that she understood the situation so perfectly.

'That's just what happened. Ros had had enough.'

'And you chucked us all up?'

Alex threw her hands in the air in an expansive dramatic gesture so that one or two people, who were already quite interested anyway in the drama that was obviously going on, openly stared at them.

'Oh Alex, no. Look don't make gestures like that. People will wonder what's happening. What a ridiculous thing to say. Of course I haven't chucked you all up!'

He indignantly lit a cigarette without offering Alex one and signalled for the bill, looking at his watch at the same time. Harry Twentyman, the very busy executive remembering he had to get back to the office and see an important client.

'Harry, you can't leave it like this.' Alex said with some panic recognizing the signs of Harry having had enough.

'Darling, I've got a meeting.'

'You can come and see me at the house. What about the children?'

'How *are* they, Alex?' Harry said with sudden solemnity just for the moment forgetting the meeting. In his eyes she saw the concern of the man she used to know; the Harry who cared. She saw then the man she loved, still did as much as ever – the tender, caring, personal Harry, not the man of affairs. She wanted Harry to say that all this had been stupid, he felt as she did and he would come home with her. She returned his look with a lingering one of her own until he lowered his eyes and she knew he would not come back, just yet.

'How do you think? They're very upset of course. I told them you'd stayed in France, but Portia learned the truth from Emma and Roger and passed it on.'

'Hell.'

'Well, I think they could tell. I mean I tried, but I wasn't myself. God almighty, Harry, what *did* you expect? That I could just go on as though nothing had happened? One moment we have a perfectly happy, normal home of four people, a cat and six goldfish and the next it is shattered and split into thousands of tiny fragments. Suddenly it is not a home at all but a place full of misery. And it is all *your* fault, Harry, and you have the nerve to say . . .'

Alex was trembling so much that her voice shook, she knew it. There was a tight, constricting feeling in her head and a sort of red blur in front of her eyes. Maybe she was going to have a stroke? *That* would teach him. She waited to topple over in some kind of fit or faint, but nothing so obliging happened. Harry always said she was so strong, so hale and healthy.

'Alex!' Harry hissed, lowering his voice and glancing around uncomfortably again. 'Don't be so *dramatic*! There is nothing to be gained by losing your temper. I shall just get up and walk out. If you can't be civilized . . .'

Civilized. It was a useful term. It meant not saying what you felt; not showing hurt; not scratching people's eyes out when they behaved badly. She and Harry were very civilized people. It was expected. Alex swallowed.

'It's hard not to say what I feel. You seem to have no idea.'

'Of course I have, Alex.' Harry, smiling understandingly, put a hand protectively over hers. 'I am not a cruel man. In fact it is because I am not cruel that I simply couldn't tell you; didn't want to hurt you. Rosalind has been asking me to for months. But I couldn't.'

'But, Harry, there never even seemed any strain in our relationship. That's the part I can't understand. Or am I so very thick? You seemed just the same as always to me.'

'Yes I was. I am. I mean I did love you, Alex, and do. I love the kids.'

'You would be perfectly happy with two wives?'

Harry smiled; that chuckling nautical smile she loved so much.

'I could be happy with either. Yes.'

'Even if I said you could go on with Rosalind would you come home?'

Harry stared at her; the smile had gone.

'Would you?'

'I think I would. Hoping things would sort themselves out. I'm not saying *I* could feel the same. I'm thinking mainly of the children. I'd be hoping, of course that you would tire of Rosalind. Would you, Harry, come home?'

Harry bowed his head.

'I don't know. It would cause one hell of a stink with her. No, I've made the break, Alex; just for now . . . making the break was the hard part and I've done it.'

'For ever, Harry?'

'I don't know, Alex. Look, I'm glad we had this talk. It has cleared things.'

'When will you come and see the children?'

Alex hadn't thought anything had been cleared. A good bit of it was waffle, the rest she still didn't understand.

'*Very* soon. And I will keep in touch, Alex. I haven't gone forever. I mean I'll always be about.'

'I think you owe it to the children to explain things to them, Harry.'

But if Harry had found it so difficult to explain things to her, how could she possibly expect him to be brave enough to explain it to young trusting minds?

She felt a kind of despair now as though she had gambled on this meeting being productive, solving something, and had lost.

For Harry seemed to have evaporated as a personality; there was an evasiveness about him with which she was completely unfamiliar. It certainly hadn't been there before, or she hadn't noticed it. If he'd been deceiving her for over a year, you would have thought you would have detected some change in his behaviour.

But Alex hadn't. Had she been too complacent, too satisfied, too over-confident, too obtuse to notice she had lost her husband's complete affection – and was that the reason she had?

6

Alex thought that, in different circumstances, she might rather have liked Rosalind Vaughan. Maybe it was a question of like attracting like because, as Emma had suggested, they resembled each other. Although Rosalind's hair was darker than Alex's, straighter, not as thick, they both had deep blue eyes, clear complexions, full sensual mouths and good bone structure. Rosalind was about half a head shorter than Alex, but managed to appear taller in her high heels as she walked without a trace of nerves, quite boldly in fact, into Alex's sitting room and looked round for somewhere to sit.

That Rosalind was here at all was due to a last desperate attempt on Alex's part to get some sort of sense into the situation. Alex knew that Rosalind was the key to Harry, the only way to get at him because he had steadily refused to see her again since their meeting at Luigi's. At first it hadn't been an obvious refusal, merely a series of postponements. Then he had agreed to meet the children at the Draxes. It would be 'better' he said, less emotional.

What Alex didn't know was the part Rosalind had played in all this though she'd had a good guess. Rosalind Vaughan, on hearing an amused Harry tell her that his wife was quite content to have him at home and countenance a mistress, had made up her mind on the spot. Any woman who would suggest such an extraordinary compromise must be desperate. To let Harry near Alex would be fatal. So she had more or less forbidden Harry to go to his home without her and by this time Harry, still surprised at the ease with which she had taken over his life, decided to do what he was told by someone who was so obviously much stronger than either Alex or himself.

This continual non-communication with Harry, except in

brief conversations on the phone, Alex found very hard to cope with. The new evasiveness of Harry was so difficult to understand; never 'yes' or 'no', but 'maybe' or 'sometime'. Harry was almost off-hand as though the whole thing was of not much consequence, quite forgetting or ignoring his promises in the restaurant. Except that he didn't actually live there, he told her, nothing had changed. He was still fond of her, the children; he hadn't cut her allowance, she had the house. Yes of course he would discuss things; soon.

But that day never came. In the end Alex herself told the children that Daddy was living away from home for reasons she didn't understand. Already she could sense a withdrawal from her, especially on Toby's part, a suspicion that it was some fault of hers that the much-beloved parent was missing from home.

One or two of the people within her confidence – and there were few of these, Natasha Pont was one – suggested a lawyer, but Alex felt this would antagonize Harry in a way she had so far avoided. A lawyer had seemed a terribly final step to Alex, one she shrank from. A lawyer was like a declaration of war, whereas she was trying to maintain a state of skirmish. The children began to look forward to seeing their father with an enthusiasm Alex thought excessive. Perhaps his rarity value made him more appreciated, and their attitude to their mother changed because she was the one they saw all the time, who gave tickings-off and administered punishment. For his part Daddy took on a sort of invisible heroic role because seeing him was associated with something nice, outings, lots of kisses, cuddles, and sometimes presents. Then there was this awfully nice lady with him who was a lot of fun too, always smiling whereas Mummy smiled so little these days. In fact, Alex felt she was carrying a great deal and the strain showed in insomnia, tiredness and frequent visits to the doctor who prescribed tranquillizers, anti-depressants and sleeping pills. Alex now had a little stack of bottles by her bedside where before she had merely had a good book and the alarm clock. The latter was necessary no more. If Alex slept through the night at all she awoke with the the birds and lay waiting for the light to break so that she could get up and move around – to forget.

By December Alex had accepted the fact that she was on

the brink of losing control of herself, and the situation was impossible. She could hardly recognize the person she was three months ago, as she could hardly recognize her husband, or her children. In such a short time everything had changed. It was alarming to find oneself so vulnerable to circumstances and one wondered how one would cope with death, or any other major upheaval; but then the disruption of a tranquil home life was like a death and was also a major upheaval as her doctor had frequently pointed out.

Alex had finally lured Rosalind to the house by threatening to come to the office to make a scene. She'd phoned Rosalind when she knew Harry was in Germany and Rosalind for some reason hadn't gone with him; perhaps she felt so secure now she didn't need to. Rosalind had at first refused a meeting then, on hearing Alex's threat, suggested a restaurant; but Alex had said her home or Rosalind's and Rosalind quickly agreed to come to Bonnington Crescent at eleven in the morning.

Alex had coffee ready and firm *langues de chat* which she baked herself. On the other hand, she wasn't going to behave or dress differently in any way for Rosalind. After all, she was the wounded party; Rosalind the aggressor. She wore her faded blue denims and a velour tee shirt with long sleeves which she hitched half-way up her arms because it was a cold day and she had turned the central heating up.

Rosalind had on a beige woollen two-piece, and high heeled brown calf shoes with matching handbag. She'd driven herself over in Harry's Volvo and wore no coat. Alex noticed she wore no rings and was glad she had kept her wedding ring on. After all, as far as she was concerned, she was still married to Harry. It was just a thin gold band but rather loose now on her finger because she had lost weight.

'Is this supposed to be some confrontation?' Rosalind said, sitting down and elegantly crossing her rather good legs. 'I mean we might as well come to the point.'

'At least have some coffee?' Alex said pleasantly, but boiling inwardly at the rudeness of the opening remark.

'Thanks. Black please.'

Alex passed her coffee in the thin, Royal Doulton porcelain cup.

'Biscuit?'

'No thanks.'

Alex added milk to her own coffee and took it to the sofa facing Rosalind. She was surprised to find she was still cold and the exposed flesh on her arms was covered in goose pimples. Nerves probably.

'No it's not a confrontation. I've tried for nearly three months to be very reasonable; to try and understand. I've even done my best to find out what Harry has in mind. I don't think you can blame me for this. But I can't find out anything, I can't get anywhere. Our lives have been completely disrupted and at the moment I can't even see any conclusion.'

Rosalind, she saw, was watching her keenly. She had a very direct look, an intelligent expression that was not unattractive. She tipped her head on one side and seemed to be giving Alex her whole, not unsympathetic, attention. Alex thought she'd matured since she'd last seen her. When Alex stopped talking Rosalind didn't immediately speak, considering her words. When she spoke she looked at Alex straight in the eyes.

'It's been very hard for Harry too. Harry feels it a lot more keenly than you appear to think. No don't laugh, Mrs Twentyman,' Rosalind put out an elegant hand in warning. 'Harry has been very unhappy and bewildered. He's avoided meeting you because he doesn't know what to say. It's just as simple as that.'

'But don't you think Harry has a *duty*?' Alex said quietly noting the 'Mrs Twentyman'. Right, it was going to be that sort of relationship. 'A duty to do the right thing, to discuss things, even if he wanted to leave home? Not leave just a void?'

'Harry didn't want to leave home. I thought you knew that.'

Rosalind's eyes flashed as though she was aware that now she had entered dangerous waters.

'You made him, in other words.'

'Mrs Twentyman, you know that you can't make a person do something they don't really want to do. Nothing I could have said or done would have taken Harry away if he didn't really ultimately want to go. You know it takes two to break a marriage.'

'Three,' Alex said shortly. 'Don't forget yourself.'

A faint flush suffused Rosalind's cheeks which Alex thought

wasn't solely due to the heat.

'I just helped him to make up his mind. Yes, I'll admit I chose the time and I made it difficult for him; but I don't own Harry any more than you did and he had a choice. I was quite prepared for him to come back here when we returned, but he didn't. You see for too long Harry had had it both ways. A nice home, children, attractive wife; and then a mistress, compliant, sexy, willing to fit in with all the odd hours such a relationship demands. I got tired of it and I told Harry it had to end. Although he said you hardly slept together I don't believe him, or even if it was true I didn't like the thought of him fucking us both, at any time, never mind on the same day. It's not hygienic.'

Briefly Alex shut her eyes. The pain was too intense. The sexual connotation (for some reason) was always the worst. Now she had to discuss it with his mistress.

'You were right not to believe Harry. We had a very active sex life. I thought it was a very good, important part of our marriage, and I miss it.'

Rosalind avoided looking directly at Alex for the first time and instead seemed to find something intriguing on the toes of her shoes.

'I see,' she said at last very quietly then, with a hint of admiration in her voice, 'he's a swine, isn't he? Fancy finding the energy!'

'Or the time,' Alex said drily. 'I thought he was so occupied with his business.'

'I think the business is part of the trouble. Could I have some more coffee and perhaps one of those biscuits after all?' Rosalind extended her cup with a smile. Alex could perceive a slight thaw in the atmosphere and took her cup.

'Part of what trouble?'

'Part of Harry's trouble. It hasn't been going well for a long time. Everything seemed to be falling apart for Harry, the business and his marriage. He needed someone to cling to.'

'Why not me?' Alex returned the cup and offered the plate of biscuits. Rosalind bit one and looked thoughtful.

'It's very hard to say this, but I think he was ashamed of not succeeding. You see, despite what you think, he didn't really feel at ease with you, he couldn't confide in you.'

'Of course Harry could confide in me! I think he's given a very wrong impression of our marriage.'

'Of what *you* thought the marriage was, Mrs Twentyman. Harry gave me another impression.'

'What was that?'

'I think he was bored. I know that sounds hurtful and it isn't entirely your fault.'

'Thank you.'

'No, don't be sarcastic. Harry was bored with domesticity; with dinner at seven and taking the children in the park at weekends, maybe even with making love to the same woman every night. He was bored with going to the office and coming back. Harry wanted something new in his life, an excitement. Maybe what Harry wanted *was* a casual affair, but he chose the wrong girl.' Rosalind got up and moved with her back to the window so that Alex couldn't clearly see her face. 'I'd had casual affairs, plenty of them; but Harry wasn't casual for me or, rather, he was at first but it changed. I fell in love with him. I also thought he needed me. I've got a good head. I was in the wine business before and I know a lot about it. I could see what was going wrong because Harry and Roger were taken in by the old-boy network of the wine trade. Too many boozy lunches clouding their judgement.

'They invested very heavily in claret and then the bottom of the market fell through the floor. They were buying too many high-priced wines, only catering for the upper end of the trade. But a lot of people are drinking wine and I've tried to get Harry and Roger to see this, to cater for the supermarkets, the chainstores and so on.'

'You're a proper little all-rounder, aren't you?' Alex couldn't help the sarcasm in her voice. Not only had she apparently failed Harry as a wife and lover, she didn't know the first thing about the wine business.

'Don't be bitter, Mrs Twentyman. I just wanted to show you that it's more than a casual affair, more than sex. It's a kind of marriage too.'

'But we've got children. Don't you want children?'

Rosalind got out a cigarette case from her bag and offered it to Alex. Alex saw that it was new and expensive. A present from Harry no doubt. She took one and lit Rosalind's before her own.

'No I don't want children,' Rosalind said, 'to answer the last part first. I've never been interested in them and I don't want any.'

'Does Harry know this?'

'Oh yes, and I think it's part of my attraction. You see, Mrs Twentyman, Harry is a different person from the one you were used to.'

'You mean he doesn't *like* the children?'

'No. He loves them; but he didn't want any more. He said you wanted two more. It was stifling him.'

'I didn't exactly press them on Harry,' Alex said quietly; feeling indignation now, a growing sense of frustration and injury that Rosalind knew so much that Alex considered intimate between Harry and herself. 'I was prepared to wait.'

'Well Harry didn't want them at all, now or later. He knew you had it in the back of your mind and he'd have to give in; sooner or later there would be another baby and Harry didn't want one. He wants me to be a companion, a business partner. We're going to travel a lot together and I'm going to be a director of the firm.'

'Oh.'

Alex felt plain and stupid and inadequate – pale beside this Amazon who was so good at everything; sex and business and managing Harry. If Harry had really wanted this why hadn't she known? She was staring at Rosalind's legs, imagining them bare and apart, raised so often to receive Harry. Or maybe they had some terribly sophisticated positions that more than likely involved Rosalind getting on top of Harry, where she clearly was mentally and intended to stay.

'Mrs Twentyman,' Rosalind said gently bending towards the vanquished wife. 'I would so like us all to be friends, eventually. Is it possible?'

Alex wanted to scream that no it wasn't possible, likely or even desirable but she thought she'd been diminished enough by Harry's mistress. There were only a few shreds of pride left and these she must hang on to.

'Well, it's not possible while Harry doesn't talk; when he won't see me and the children.'

'But he *does* see the children. Almost every week he picks

them up at the Draxes and then we take them somewhere for the day. We have a lovely time. Surely you know that?'

'Yes but don't you see it's alienating the children from me? They think I'm to blame for their father leaving. Now they associate him only with good and nice things and me with the bad and unpleasant. I've less time for them. I'm much more nervous and irritable. I've changed for the worse. I was quite unprepared for what happened. I knew nothing about you. Can't you understand *that*?'

Alex felt she was betraying too much emotion when, in front of this woman, Harry's mistress, she so desperately wanted to remain self-possessed. She seemed to be pleading with her and she knew her eyes faltered under Rosalind's steady gaze.

'I'm very sorry,' Rosalind said quietly. 'I really am. I didn't see it from the point of view of the children. Harry always said you were so capable and collected. I don't think he ever thought it would affect you in this way or your relationship with Toby and Rachel. I suppose it was stupid of us not to realize it. But you see, Mrs Twentyman, Harry knows you want him back. That's why he avoids the house. He knows you love him. I know it too. I know you were prepared to share him with me . . .'

Alex felt her face sting with a sudden hot flush. There was absolutely nothing this girl didn't know.

'Well . . . I don't think I feel that now. It was said weeks ago in an emotional moment. It would be much more natural if we met here. If Harry picked them up and brought them back and didn't treat me like some kind of pariah. The kids feel it. I promise I won't lay a hand on him.'

Now it was Rosalind's turn to redden and avoid Alex's eyes.

'That's ridiculous. I don't think that at all. But I will speak to Harry about this. It seems reasonable to me.'

Harry's keeper, granting a concession, Alex thought, hating the person. In the silence that followed Rosalind took up her bag from the sofa where she'd left it.

'For everyone's sake we must try and be reasonable, Mrs Twentyman, for the children first and foremost. Why should they suffer? Believe me, Harry did think of the children all the time. But what he did was bound to hurt someone. These things do hurt, you know.'

'I hope they hurt you one day,' Alex said getting to her feet. 'I really hope that one day you too know what it's like.'

But looking at her she thought she wouldn't. Rosalind, unlike Alex, would know well in advance the way things were going. Rosalind would take precautions to avoid being hurt.

The clock in the hall struck twelve. They'd only been talking for an hour after all. What had been achieved? Had anything really happened? She couldn't let Rosalind go without knowing.

'Are you going to marry Harry?'

Rosalind looked surprised as though she hadn't thought about it.

'Eventually I suppose, but it's not uppermost in my mind or his; but what I do think for your own sake is important, Mrs Twentyman, is that you realize Harry has left you and that, at the moment anyway as far as I can see, he has not the slightest intention of coming back. I think when you accept that you'll feel better. You're a very lovely woman. Look about you. Change your life. Find a man who will give you the children you want; the kind of life you like.'

'I thought I had,' Alex said. 'How will I know that I'm right the second time when I was so wrong once?'

'That's a chance we all have to take,' Rosalind shrugged. 'Believe me I am sorry; but I think it was inevitable. If not with me, Harry would have gone off with someone else. I just don't think you're his sort of woman. You're much too domestic and maternal for Harry.'

'We know two different men, you and I. You realize that, don't you?' Alex said accompanying her to the hall. She didn't want Rosalind to go now; she wanted this one link with Harry to stay.

'Yes, completely; but I don't think Harry is schizo and I've been working for him for nearly two years. I think I know him very well, and the brief time we've been living together confirms this. Look, I know Harry has avoided lawyers and that kind of thing. He does tend to shirk the issues; he does it in business too. I'll try and get him to have a proper settlement drawn up, about the house and so on. But I must warn you, Harry has got very little money. We are all going to have to work extremely hard to survive. Harry has avoided telling you this, but it's absolutely essential that you know.'

'What?'

'Your whole life-style has got to change. You're going to have to economize, cut corners, take a job. The economic situation is going to get worse. The bad time is only just beginning.'

And in this, as in so much else, Rosalind Vaughan proved right.

Part Two

The Women

7

Alex stood in the playground of the Princess Maud Junior School and looked up at the ugly late Victorian building which even the soft golden light of the early September sun failed to mellow. It had been built in the last decade of the reign of Queen Victoria and named after her grand-daughter who was to marry the King of Norway. The playground was large and asphalt and not a tree or a blade of grass transformed its strict functionalism.

In the old days it had been a council school where the children largely of the poor were educated. Now it was part of the state system, a primary school for the education of boys and girls between the ages of 7 and 11.

Alex had been horrified when she'd first been taken round the Princess Maud School. Although they were no longer used, there were separate entrances for girls and boys marked in stone in italic script 'girls ', 'boys'. Stone staircases were surmounted by white stone tiles and the whole place, with many floors, corridors and unrelated parts seemed to have been designed by some mad architect.

Alex had compared this utilitarian building devoid of all charm or warmth with the convent, housed in what had once been a large gracious Victorian mansion set in acres of parkland in Hampstead with a pond on which beautiful white swans swam elegantly up and down. Why, even the drive up to the school was a quarter of a mile long and inside everything was polished wood and brass, smelling of beeswax and incense.

Or The Heath, the private school where Toby had gone to prepare him for public school, that was even grander than the convent being a purpose-built modern building, low and set among trees and lawns with a view over Hampstead Heath as far as the City of London. Every facility was available there, every sport from croquet to cricket.

But Alex had had no option. The very last thing she had wanted to do was to change the children's schools; already with their lives so disrupted she had at least wanted to leave them that. At such an impressionable time for their worlds to collapse, all their security to vanish . . . it was too much. Everyone told her children were resilient, but Alex remembered her own secure, happy childhood and thought that if, with all that behind her, she found it now so hard to cope, what would happen to her children in later life? In the difficult times they were bound to have, how would they react if their happy secure world was in pieces now?

Rosalind's visit in December the year before had indeed performed one important function; nothing pleasant had actually happened, but Harry had at least agreed to meet her at her lawyer's and a settlement of separation had been worked out which impressed the lawyer as a demonstration of Harry's goodwill. Most wives weren't nearly so lucky he had assured her. Oh no, when she tried to argue, not even when the circumstances had been like hers and many were. She wasn't unique. Why some apparently contented men disappeared altogether, just walked out and were never heard from or seen again. No, even the happiest marriages, he assured her. Yes, most extraordinary.

Harry had agreed to let her keep the house, for the time being; it was the matrimonial home and he couldn't really break it up without a struggle; but her allowance had to be reduced. The economic crisis had begun fully to grip the country; overdrafts were being curtailed, borrowing for investment became practically impossible for the small under-capitalized business. Hundreds were going bust, especially in a business like Harry's where you had to invest a lot in the first place before you began to see results. Alex started to hear a great deal about a hitherto unfamiliar term: cash flow. Apparently what you were expecting wasn't the important thing; it was what you had to spend or live on *now* and, when it came to it, Harry had very little. His comfortable life-style had largely been based on credit.

But Rosalind wasn't the rat to cling to the sinking ship. No indeed. She loved Harry and she wanted him, but not as a desperate out-of-work character. That would change his desirability completely. Here was a man with a fine physique, charm, experience and good in bed; he must be successful too. She must make him successful so that they could enjoy the good life together. And the good life didn't lie in her bachelor flat in Earl's Court.

So Harry and Rosalind wanted to move and Harry had to pay the new mortgage. Rosalind of course wanted her savings left where they were, in shares, though the stock market had taken a battering too. The only way for Harry to get a second house mortgage and survive was to raise more capital, and the only way he could do this was to sell much of the valuable antique furniture with which the Twentyman house had been furnished. Alex had to agree to this; she had no option and almost in a day the Georgian and Victorian cupboards, tables and escritoires went out and some functional good modern furniture, very little of it, from Heal's moved in. The large Victorian bed stayed though, goodness knows, she felt lonely enough in it.

Then the schools. Great economies were to be made there so that Harry and Rosalind could buy the convenient box near the river in Putney they felt would suit them for the time being.

Harry's lawyer and Alex's lawyer nearly came to blows about the schools – so Alex's lawyer told her or pretended – but Harry was being so very generous in everything else that he advised her to give in. But when Alex came to broach it to Toby and Rachel that they might have to leave they didn't appear too put out. She then discovered that children whose parents were both hard up and living apart were somehow singled out at the prep school, but especially at the convent. The children knew; it got around and, whereas many of their parents were divorced, they had managed so far to avoid the stigma of being broke too. As long as there was no difficulty paying the fees all was well.

But Harry refused to pay the fees and wrote and told the Reverend Mother and the Head of The Heath school so. He said they would be the responsibility of his wife and Alex had a painful interview with Reverend Mother, who would have made an excellent businesswoman had she chosen the secular life. She said that she was sorry to hear about the Twentymans' difficulties but Rachel's work had dropped off, and she no longer seemed to get on as well as she had with the other girls. She sulked and cried a lot, no longer benefited from the school as she had. Yes, Reverend Mother was very sorry but, she seemed to say, her head on one side, the white coif emphasizing her soft unlined face, if parents kept the commands of God and stayed together this sort of thing wouldn't happen, would it?

The Head of The Heath was much more perfunctory, less imbued with the spirit of Christian charity. No fees, no school; there were bursaries for deserving cases, but it seemed to him that Mr Twentyman could afford to pay but didn't want to. Sorry. Out.

Alex who had to endure these interviews on her own reached a level of humiliation she had never imagined possible. She avoided the other mothers and there were few invitations to tea in the summer term, though one or two of the mothers, such as Natasha Pont, whom she had least expected to understand, were supportive.

Emma Drax continued supportive too, despite the fact that there was the difficulty of Roger. Roger clearly wanted to be on the winning side which he took to be that of Harry and Rosalind, and anyway Rosalind was saving the business with her expertise and the range of her contacts in the trade. He didn't want to be involved with Alex or see her if possible; so Emma stopped asking Alex to dinner and had her to coffee instead.

Alex noticed it; but she had noticed a lot of things since she had been single, such as that your evening invitations dropped almost to nil and also that however much you looked about for a man there didn't seem to be any around. How did you meet them? You couldn't just fling yourself into groups and evening classes, join clubs or societies. In the first place there was the baby-sitting problem; they were difficult to get, expensive and you couldn't possibly leave two suddenly rather disturbed youngsters on their own. Then there was the problem of being constantly tired because of your bad nights and, to be truthful, you didn't want to anyway; prowling around scouring the halls of London for men.

After Christmas when the first stages in the settlement were being reached (the fight about the schools was still to come) Alex decided to let the basement flat, empty since Harry's mother had died. She thought she would let it to men and see what happened. In stories in women's magazines romantic attachments were always starting that way. Someone in the basement flat or across the road. Usually handsome, virile, with lots of charm.

But when Harry heard what she had in mind he warned her to be careful (about the letting, that is, she didn't say she was trying to find a lover too). Now, because of the Rent Act, you couldn't get people out once you had them in, no not even in furnished places; no, no matter how clever you were. The best way was to get tenants through an agency that specialized in short-term lettings, people from abroad.

Alex watched the unending succession of short-term tenants come and go – Japanese, Indian, Portuguese, American. Monied and polite, careful and quiet but always couples; it was such a small flat after all. At Easter two men finally arrived for a two month stay, but although attractive and courteous they seemed extraordinarily attached to each other and Alex was quite shocked to discover by chance that the second bedroom was unslept in and they shared a bed. After the lovers finally went back to the U.S.A. there was a South American diplomat with a fierce expression and twirling moustaches. He kept on bringing boxes in and out of the house and Alex became convinced he was an urban guerrilla and was busy making bombs or planning to hijack aeroplanes. In the end he left suddenly and without saying goodbye, so perhaps she was right. He had paid for the flat until September so she decided to have a rest and not to let it.

But all this was as nothing to the problem of finding a job. She'd been a highly trained, well-paid secretary, the sort that Rosalind was now, or rather had been before her elevation. But after twelve years she discovered that she had few of her old skills left. Her typing was slow, her shorthand erratic and her book-keeping knowledge nil. Also there were all the new fangled taxes, VAT and such like.

Besides, there were the hours. She wanted to be home for her children, who were having a bad enough time as it was without a father and an unhappy school life. She was their one security, their anchor. She must not fail them. And then there were the holidays; what did you do about that? She had no money so she couldn't afford an au pair, and no relatives who would easily take the children. Mrs Buchanan, still ignorant in the Isle of Mull about what was happening to her daughter, suffered from arthritis and was often bedridden. She couldn't skip up and down to help out.

Emma Drax had told her quite frankly that she ought to have a chat with the Social Security people, but the very idea horrified Alex. She was too middle-class, too independent to want to be an entry in the welfare system of the State.

She looked for work in the *Ham and High* advertisement pages and endured a number of lifeless jobs in small offices where she crouched by an electric fire and typed on an ancient Underwood, or filed depressing invoices for hours on end. Part-time jobs it seemed were all like this; they were badly paid and boring, but there were enough needy housewives like her to take them.

By the summer Alex was more exhausted than ever, but at least things were beginning to straighten out. Harry and Rosalind had their Putney house and now came regularly to Bonnington Crescent together to fetch Toby and Rachel for the day every other Sunday. Harry was never allowed to be alone with Alex; Rosalind watched him like a hawk. Alex noticed they had also managed to buy a new expensive car. The very sight of their happiness and prosperity gave her nausea and she tried to be polite but brief when she saw them. She also knew that she looked tired and haggard compared to the blooming Rosalind who had new blonde streaks in her hair.

Also by the summer the school business was sorted out (Harry had agreed to pay the fees until then) and the children didn't seem as worried by the drabness of the Princess Maud School as Alex was, but appeared to like the young energetic headmaster, to approve the idea of not wearing uniform and to welcome the atmosphere of boys and girls mixed.

Toby had been especially difficult during the summer term. He had started coming to her bed at night and though his firm little body sometimes comforted her, she thought it was wrong in principle that a boy of 10 should start sleeping with his mother. Toby had never been a one for coming to their bed.

It was for this reason, as well as her moments of panic and

apparent inability to adjust, that Alex had agreed to see Emma's psychiatrist, whom she familiarly referred to as 'Dick' having, by now, known him for so long. 'Just for a few chats darling,' Emma had suggested. Alex had turned to Dick with something like relief, a strong professional man to talk to. But the image that had been conjured up by Emma did not square with the facts. 'Dick' was in fact Dr Frank Dickson, a member of the Royal College of Psychiatrists, and the trendy image – Alex had imagined a beard and jeans and sandals, perhaps a few beads – became instead a tall distinguished looking man with pince-nez and a pin-striped suit. He had a comfortable consulting room attached to his house in Maida Vale and Alex lay on his long, low couch and parted with all her secrets, laid bare her inner self. She talked and talked and now and then Dr Dickson murmured from his seat at the back of her head; but somehow it did her good. It seemed to work. He didn't try and explain her or Harry but to get her to explain events herself, see why it had all gone wrong and how much of it was Harry's fault and how much hers.

Over the months Alex found that she sounded like a tiresome repetitive gramophone record, accusing Harry all the time so that a picture emerged of someone who was almost too good to be true: herself. After a good weep in front of Dr Dickson a more realistic picture had begun to emerge of a woman who had expected and demanded perfection in herself and everyone else; who had never deviated from the bright shining path that led to true happiness, she'd thought; who had never lost control except in bed where it was expected and therefore permissible.

'You see,' Dr Dickson volunteered in one of his rare comments, barely audible, 'you had become pretty impossible to keep up with.'

Impossible? *Her*?

* * *

Rosalind and Harry had gone away with the Draxes for the summer holiday which Alex thought was tactless. Emma had been too embarrassed to mention it and they just took off. Alex gave up her latest temporary job and took the children up to her parents where at last she told them the truth.

The Buchanans weren't half as upset as Alex had feared they would be. In fact she found they knew a good deal more about life than she'd imagined. They rallied round with practical help and advice and were only distressed she hadn't told them sooner. But more importantly they begged her to leave the children with them and she went on a tour of Scotland and the Lakes by herself, staying at comfortable hotels, eating well and sleeping, oh sleeping.

She even had an affair; the story-book thing where there is an attractive man at the next table on his own. He was an American and, although he was on his own, he was on his way back to Houston where he had a wife. He was in oil and had been visiting the rigs in the North Sea. He was gentle and charming and they spent an idyllic few days together and he helped to restore to Alex some of her lost confidence in herself, showed her she wasn't dry and sterile and sexually dead as she'd thought.

Alex returned with the children to London at the end of August with the glimmerings of a positive attitude about the future.

* * *

She'd taken Rachel and Toby in to meet their form teachers and watched the nice looking crowd of youngsters who teemed into the school on that first day of term, most of them greeting old friends, some shy and quiet as Toby and Rachel had been. There were a few parents left in the playground with her, standing isolated, looking up at the school as she was, mostly mothers. Some had babies in prams, some a smaller child, but most were on their own.

Alex wondered how many of them were on their own completely. Women like her? She turned away and got into the car left outside the school gate. She would soon find out.

8

Lorna Galbraith hurried away from the college in order to be at the school by half past three. Two days a week she could get off early and she liked to pick up the children herself and if possible invite their special friends for tea.

Sally had taken a great shine to a new girl in her class, Rachel Twentyman, and it was Rachel's turn to come to tea. Lorna had spoken to her mother on the phone and thought she sounded a nice woman, possibly a recruit for the parents' committee.

Lorna was always in a hurry; there were ten thousand things to do and never enough time in which to do them. She never considered that she made things happen so as not to have a vacuum for a minute. She was just one of nature's busy people; had a busy life and a busy husband who was always, but always away.

Lorna screamed round the corner in her Mini and parked on the pavement outside the school; there was the usual crush of traffic and swarming people. Sally was there with her gang of friends and beside her stood one of the most beautiful children Lorna had ever seen – petite, fragile, with olive skin and limpid brown eyes. She looked shy and withdrawn and not at all Sally's type. Fragile people always made Lorna rather nervous, and she approached her daughter and her guest with caution.

'Mum, this is Rachel,' Sally shouted, forcing Rachel forward. A tall blond boy, not a bit like the little girl, stood beside her protectively and smiled at Lorna.

'I'm Rachel's brother, Toby Twentyman. Mum said to see she got off all right. Mum will pick her up at six-thirty if that is all right.'

'Of course, Toby, and what will you do?'

'I can take myself home thank you, Mrs Galbraith. I get a bus up the road to Swiss Cottage.'

Lorna thought he had beautiful manners; not that you'd call the kids here rough – after all it was supposed to be one of the best parts of London – but Toby's politeness was exceptional.

'How do you like the school, Toby? This is the first term for both of you, isn't it?'

'Yes.' She thought she detected a blush on the handsome face. 'Yes, I was at The Heath before.'

The Heath was the most expensive, and the most snobbish, school in North London. Lorna who detested selection and private education felt her gorge rise.

'The *Heath*?'

'Yes,' Toby looked apologetic. 'We like it here. It's different.'

'I should think it is.'

Lorna wondered what kind of parents sent a child to The Heath. Yes, there had been an upper class edge to Mrs Twentyman's voice – there was to Lorna's too, but she wasn't aware of it.

'Mummy can't stand private schools,' Sally explained, 'she's a socialist.'

Toby nodded, not quite sure what a socialist was. The Twentymans' house was particularly apolitical.

'It's a good school. They had a good cricket team. But this is all right.' Toby jerked his head backwards. 'I'll see you again, Mrs Galbraith.' He looked anxiously at his sister, waved and sloped off towards the High Street. He really was a very attractive boy.

Lorna left the girls talking while she busied off, accosting several of the mothers about the next Parents' Evening she was organizing. They were to have a talk on education by a junior member of the Government, a move that had annoyed the headmaster who wanted the school to remain unpolitical. But one thing that Lorna Galbraith felt quite prejudiced and adamant about was state education and she would ram it down the throats of everyone whether they agreed with her or not.

She eventually returned and propelled the girls into the back of the Mini and lurched off towards St John's Wood where the Galbraiths had a large untidy house full of hamsters, gerbils, rats and mice because Lorna was a behavioural psychologist who deduced much about human nature from the behaviour of these small furry creatures, rather as, all those years ago, Pavlov had with his dogs. It was amazing the amount they could teach you. Lorna had two other children at the local Comprehensive school, of which she was a governor, and they found their own way home. Her boy Douglas would be a bit older than Toby Twentyman, she decided. She should bring them together so that Douglas could brainwash Toby out of the unfortunate influence of his private school. The Heath indeed!

George Galbraith was away, as he nearly always was, so she ran her Mini into the garage and took the girls into the house through the side door. Inside was a state of chaos that quite shocked Rachel who had hardly ever seen an untidy house in her life; certainly not one like this.

There were animal cages all over the floor of the large kitchen, papers on the floor, the table, everywhere and an enormous pile of washing up in the sink. In a far corner huddled a disgruntled pile of dirty clothes. The place also smelt. Rachel wished she'd never let Mummy accept the invitation for her. She didn't even like Sally Galbraith much anyway; she was far too boisterous and bossy, worse than Portia Drax who had turned very funny in the summer term at the convent.

However, giving Rachel no time for reflection, Sally seized her by the hand and took her up through a hall overflowing with plants, papers and more furry animals in cages, up some uncarpeted stairs to a playroom where there was more chaos but at least no animals. There was an unmade bunk bed and, from drawers and cupboards books, toys, lengths of material and clothes spilled in cornucopic profusion.

'Let's dress up!' Sally exclaimed excitedly and began burrowing in a chest whose lid would not close.

Meanwhile downstairs Lorna was going through the second post. The usual bills they never paid until final reminders came in, notices of meetings, academic journals and a letter from George to say he was staying in the States a further three months.

'Christ!' Lorna exclaimed aloud. Did the man not want to come home? She might as well be a single parent for all the help she got from him. She hurled herself on to the telephone to convey to as many people as possible, in the short time available, this latest outrage on the part of her errant spouse.

When Alex got to the house in St John's Wood she was at first taken aback by the size of it in such an expensive part of London. It lay off one of the main roads leading to the park. Alex was quite used to splendid houses in Hampstead, but this . . .

However when the front door opened eventually, first to her ringing and then banging when she discovered the bell didn't work, she thought the inside looked like the emanation of some gothic nightmare. The parquet floor of the hall was scratched and unpolished and there was no carpet on the stairs. Lorna had put on a pair of slacks that were too large for her, and two enormous breasts bounced loosely against the almost transparent cheesecloth garment she wore on her upper half. Alex could clearly see the outlines of huge dark splayed nipples through the garment and the deep cleavage between the mountainous breasts.

However, above this untidy and faintly nauseating sight a pleasant enough face looked out, bright, attractive and even fairly youthful, although she was older than Alex, around 40 maybe. She had long dark hair tied back by a very tatty black ribbon, and two enormous brass earrings, full like the pendulous breasts, dangled from lobes that seemed to find the weight almost too much to bear.

She was a very odd looking creature, Alex thought. Unusual; she'd never seen anything quite like her.

'Mrs Twentyman? Come in. The kids are having a marvellous time upstairs. Rachel was rather shy at first; she is shy, isn't she? But such a lovely girl, and your son so handsome. Douglas my middle son, is 12. I wondered if Toby would come and play with him? My eldest, Rufus, is going up to Oxford next year. Yes, quite a gap, but my husband is hardly ever at home. People say it's a wonder we ever managed to breed at all. Do come in.'

Alex, feeling already breathless at the onslaught and cold because, during it, she had been standing on the doorstep, stepped inside. To her surprise she was led into a large tidy sitting room lined with rows of books and illuminated by soft, gentle lighting. It was such a contrast to the impression she'd received in the hall that she stood still for a moment so that her hostess behind her nearly cannoned into her.

'Oops sorry. I know, you've had a surprise. Everyone has. But George says we must have one tidy place in the house and it is this. He insists and I agree with him, for once!'

Lorna gave a hearty laugh and switched off the television set.

'I always like the news. Would you have a drink? I've started I'm afraid. Tuesday always wears me out. I have to lecture twice to undergraduates and it always exhausts me. They're so inattentive or lazy or both.'

'You're a lecturer?' It had seemed obvious now, given the bookshelves. The Twentymans just had one rather small bookcase mainly full of book club editions.

'I'm a psychologist, behavioural, why people do this and that.'

'Oh.' Alex couldn't help wondering why Mrs Galbraith looked as she did in that case, because if she tucked her large bust in a bra and wore clothes that fitted her, she would look quite attractive. She was very overweight but she had beautiful hair, clear skin and good bone structure.

Lorna was surprised by Alex; not quite what she'd expected from the phone. She was a pretty but rather vulnerable looking woman, uncertainty about her brilliant blue eyes. She was dressed neatly in black slacks, a black top, and a raincoat. Lorna had meant to launch straight into an attack on private education, but something about Mrs Twentyman made her desist and she'd offered her a drink instead.

The drink was very sweet vin rosé, but Alex didn't care. She'd been trying all day to get a job and found there weren't any about. People were cutting down because of the economic crisis.

'Do you do anything?' Mrs Galbraith enquired brightly, 'or are you just a mum?'

Since the break up Alex had felt very nervous about talking about herself; she even lied when she felt like it, pretending her husband was still at home. But because she felt depressed by the day and there was something kindly about this large untidy-looking woman she didn't lie.

'No, I'm a secretary, when I can get a job. They're hard to find at the moment. I like to be at home for the children.'

'Of course. I do too, and I can two days a week. I always have to box and cox about the other three. Does your husband . . .'

'My husband and I have parted,' Alex displayed her now ringless hands, rather as a cat prepares to scratch a chair. She made a habit of this whenever she told people, as though to show she was free, unencumbered.

'Oh, I'm sorry. Recently?'

Alex tilted her chin defensively. 'Yes, is it so obvious?'

'Hell no, not at all. It was just Toby, your son, said he had been at The Heath until this term. It would add up that something had happened.' Lorna couldn't help saying 'The Heath' in a tone of deep disparagement, but otherwise her voice was gentle. She refilled the glass which she saw had been drained very quickly.

'About a year,' Alex said. 'Just a year in fact. October last. My husband is in the wine business and went on a trip to France.'

'And it happened there?'

'Yes, very suddenly. I'd thought we were happily married.'

Lorna moved over to the sofa and sat next to Alex as though to offer moral support. 'You poor girl, you mean you expected nothing?'

'No.' Even after all this time Alex could hardly speak about it without crying, especially if she was tired like today.

'That's awful. With most people it's on and off for ages before the break. At least it's either mutual or usually expected. The necessary inevitable expression of disenchantment as they call it.'

'Yes I know. The irony is that Roger, my husband's partner, was the one who was always playing around. Everyone would quite have expected Roger to go, but not Harry.'

'And you still . . . feel for him?' Lorna said gently.

'Yes I do, not as much, but I still do if I'm honest. He suited me so very well, and I loved him. You can't just unlove like that, however much you want to.'

'Of course you can't.'

'And he behaved quite well . . . well,' Alex blew her nose, 'fairly well. Tried to spare me as much as he could; was decent about the house, all that. Really,' Alex blew her nose hard again,

'I can't think why I'm telling you all this, you must be bored stiff.'

'Not at all, dear, not at all. If I'd had more energy I'd have gone in for medicine and become a proper psychiatrist. But everyone said my mind was too scatty, and I was lazy. But I'm very interested in people's problems. I've problems of my own too.'

'Oh really?' Alex looked around – hadn't she said something about a George? She found, since she'd been on her own, that women with men always mentioned them in the first five minutes of a conversation, and Mrs Galbraith had been no exception.

'Well my husband is never at home. He's always abroad. We hardly have a marriage to speak of and even when he's here he's on the telex or at the office all the time. I feel I've brought up my children single-handed. The only thing with George is that there're never any financial problems. Otherwise I might as well be on my own.'

'What does he do?'

'He's a physicist; an expert on heating, industrial heating, factories and so on. He's a partner in a rather large firm of heating engineers and his work has always come first. No question.'

Lorna shook her head and refilled their glasses. 'This rosé isn't bad is it? We must save some for Fay,' she looked at the clock over the mantelpiece. 'She should be here soon to bring home Doug. He's been to her after school with Ralph Timperley, Fay's son. Fay also has a child in Mrs Richards' class, Amanda, a nice little girl. Fay's on her own too,' Lorna added, as though mentioning the existence of an unpleasant but significant disease. 'Yes that will be her. Did you hear knocking?'

Alex laughed, relaxing for the first time.

'Why don't you get your bell mended?' she said.

'George is never here and I'm much too busy to see to that kind of thing.'

* * *

Fay Timperley was a small, slightly plump but comely woman

with beautiful waving burnished hair that made her rather plain face seem unimportant. Altogether the impression she gave was of someone who was attractive and who took great care of herself. Her clothes were well chosen, her make-up exact and her general appearance such that the overall effect was very pleasing.

She looked rather defensively at Alex as though with any pretty woman she obviously sensed a rival, but gave her a quick rather bleak smile. She seemed quiet and thoughtful and was listening to Lorna's non-stop patter while appearing to take the measure of Alex with surreptitious glances.

'Fay, this is Alex,' Lorna said. 'She is the mother of Rachel, also in Amanda's class.'

'I know,' Fay nodded again, the quick defensive smile.

Alex didn't know all the children in the class and had never heard of an Amanda. She'd never noticed Fay before either. She felt that Fay wanted to be alone with Lorna, that she had something to tell her and resented finding Alex here. Alex didn't altogether take to Fay; nothing she could define exactly.

'I must go,' she said getting up. 'Toby will be home alone.'

'Bring him next time, dear, please do. Doug and Ralph have scampered upstairs without even saying hello. Sorry things are in such chaos, love. Come again soon and we'll have a long talk. I mean it. Rachel! She's a pet; Sally's mad about her. I've got your number haven't I? I'll ring soon and Toby can come to tea with Doug.'

Fay didn't come into the hall but stayed in the sitting room and Alex decided not to go in and say goodbye. She didn't feel she'd been a big hit with Fay, but she wasn't going to mind. That was one thing about the parents of the children at The Heath and the convent, there'd been no lapse of good manners. On the whole they were a lot more friendly too.

* * *

'You were cool, I thought,' Lorna said pleasantly, coming into the sitting room after Alex had left. 'Didn't you like her?'

'I thought she was cool,' Fay said, 'she gave me that disparaging look that pretty women reserve for the plain.'

'Oh Fay don't be an idiot! You're not plain. I've told you

a thousand times. You're so insecure, silly girl. Alex Twentyman is rather sweet I thought, even if she did send her kids to private schools.'

'Oh *that's* it. There's something awfully snobby about her; you can tell the way she stands apart in the playground waiting for the kids after school. I don't think she's ever noticed me. Run out of money, did they?'

'Something like that.' Lorna said, her mind preoccupied with the iniquities of private schools. 'Imagine *The Heath*! The damage it must have done to a young mind. Privilege, wealth, ostentation . . .'

Lorna rambled on, a by now quite familiar theme to Fay who only wished she'd had the chance to send her children to private schools, only she never had. It was all very well for Lorna, the product of wealth and privilege from birth, to make that sort of choice. Everyone knew the Galbraith children were bright like their parents and would do well whatever happened. If the worst did come to the worst Fay had no doubt that Lorna would hook them out of the state and into the private sector if their education really was at stake, like so many other socialists she knew.

Fay was permanently aggrieved about society and the condition in which she found herself and which she could do so little about. The world seemed a great threatening place and she was always worrying about the terrible things that were waiting for her round the corner. That's why someone like Lorna who understood was such an anchor. She'd known Lorna since the children were at the infants' school together, before Jack had left home and they still had a decent home. In a shifting, changing, hostile world Lorna, for all her faults, her inverted snobbishness and fierce prejudices, was a rock, a tower of strength.

Fay slumped into a chair and wished Lorna would shut up about private schools. The movement arrested Lorna in full flight.

'Statistics have shown that children in private schools . . . what's the matter, Fay dear. Had a bad day?'

'Yes I did have a bad day. If that man makes one more pass at me I shall have to leave. I can't bear him, but it's such a good job.'

'Then leave.'

'I don't want to. He lets me have the hours I want and it's well paid.'

'Don't you like him at all?'

'You mean I ought to go to bed with him to keep the job?'

'Of course I don't, but I just thought that maybe . . .'

Lorna looked at Fay crouched anxiously over her glass, sitting on the chair by the fireplace. Lorna, who found out everyone's business sooner or later – people tended to confide in her warm motherly amplitude – knew that the real trouble with Fay was sex. She didn't like it and never had. It was the reason Fay was always so tense and nervous like a firework squib about to go off at any second. Why she took offence so easily. It was the reason her husband Jack had finally left her and was now married again.

'He gets a hard-on just looking at me,' Fay said. 'I can see it through his trousers.'

Fay would hate this instinctive demonstration of male sexuality; it would repel her as any sexual bodily functions did – erections, lubrications, ejaculations, menstruations, emissions, having babies. The whole nasty sordid mess of sex; she wondered how anybody could like it. Lorna gazed at Fay knowing what was going on in her mind. But Fay had always refused therapy; she didn't want help even when her husband left her and took up with another woman, so what could you do about her? You couldn't *force* people, even if their marriage fell to pieces on account of some trouble that could probably be cured.

Lorna suspected Fay's hostility to her father had something to do with her attitude to men; the father who had left the mother to struggle somewhere in the north of England and bring up Fay and her three sisters. All female; left in the lurch by a man. Fay had never had a chance really; marrying the wrong man, being left by him with three children and ending up in a squalid bed-sit in Paddington before Lorna had taken charge and used her influence to get her a council flat.

You could have foretold the course of Fay's life almost from the time her father left home. Fay was one of life's victims; but what could you do about it? At least she hadn't given up completely; she took a pride in her appearance, was almost obsessively neat and well turned-out. Lucy suspected Fay would even come round to sex if she found the right man. If only she could find the right man for her, as she had helped her with so much else. The boss, nasty little Ernie Waterman, obviously wasn't the right man, and how Fay attracted them. Her very aloofness and frigidity seemed to draw men on like a charm.

'Well that's how men react if they see a desirable woman,' Lorna said trying to sound sweetly reasonable.

'It isn't. Normal men, nice men don't go round behaving like that. It's only a dirty little beast like him.'

'Try and pretend you don't notice. Get on with your typing.'

'He's always leaning up against the desk looking at me. He's rubbing it through the desk.'

Fay was almost spluttering with indignation, the very idea of the objectionable male organ getting pleasure from the sight of her.

'Fay, I think you pay too much attention to it. If you could react normally to sex it wouldn't bother you. If you could only have a proper affair with someone, or get psychiatric help as I've suggested. You've got your life in front of you, Fay, and the sort of person you are needs a man.'

'What sort of person am I then?' Fay said aggresively.

'I mean you are very womanly, defenceless. You need someone to help you, don't you? Look after you.'

Fay knew Lorna was right. She did need someone; in a way she wanted someone which was why she took such care with her appearance, tried to diet though she was naturally rather plump, took such care with her make-up. Yet the men she liked were never available, like Lorna's attractive husband George who was so charming to Fay. Fay was always attracted to unavailable men because they were no threat. The men who wanted her she shied away from, no matter what they were like. But George she liked in every way. There was a good, upright, clever man for you and though Lorna complained he was never at home, at least he was there, he was part of it. She wondered how he tolerated the mess and confusion in the home, the piles of dirty washing; he was such a neat, precise, meticulous man. There was a lot of money about too.

Fay looked about her at the subdued opulence of the Galbraiths' sitting room. Almost every object you looked at was valuable in some way. In Fay's opinion Lorna just lived in this clutter because she was ashamed of the money that enabled her to live in the best part of St John's Wood.

'I'd best get Ralph,' Fay said struggling to her feet. 'He seems to be coming along nicely with Mr Black.'

'Yes Doug likes him too.'

'I think all the children have improved in the year we've been at Emmeline Pankhurst.'

It was just good fortune that the council block where Fay and her family had been rehoused bore the name of a leading suffragette, Fay and Lorna being firm supporters of the Women's Liberation Movement. Even though it was fairly new, however, one of the criticized high-rise buildings, it was already falling to pieces. The lifts hardly ever worked, the staircase was full of rubbish and stank of urine and the garbage disposer was always blocked up. However, compared to what they'd known before, one room sharing a lavatory with ten other families in a run-down block in Paddington, it was heaven.

'You've come on too, Fay. You're not so . . . frightened.'

'Frightened? Who wouldn't have been frightened in my position? No husband, no money, the kids always ill or turning into delinquents. The number of times I had the welfare in our room I can't think. We were practically welfared out of existence, yet nothing got better. Until you got us that flat.'

She glanced gratefully at Lorna whom she so admired. Lorna's brisk thoroughness had despatched most of the welfare and procured them a large enough flat in a matter of weeks.

'Well I know about these things,' Lorna said. 'It's my profession. Don't lose your job, dear. Try and be nice to Ernie. Take no notice of the erection and maybe he'll quieten down.'

Lorna wasn't hopeful, but she was already sorting out papers for a meeting of Shelter that night. There was rarely an evening she didn't have a meeting devoted to one good work or another. The fact that her own family had to scratch around for a meal or do without was neither here nor there. Lorna never seemed to sit down to eat; she had no tranquillity. It was curious that with all her activity she managed to remain so fat.

Fay wondered if Lorna was trying to tell her she had done enough. She had found her a flat, sorted out her problems, and even found her this job. Now she was expected to keep it because she, Lorna, had moved on to other things.

'I'll drop you off,' Lorna said, 'I'm going your way. Try to get on with Mr What's-is name, Fay. Jobs are very hard to come by. Alex Twentyman was saying just that before you came.'

'She can have mine,' Fay said with a grimace. 'I'm sure Ernie wouldn't bother her at all. She looks like an easy lay . . .'

Lorna turned off the light behind them and bawled upstairs that Ralph should come down, and Doug and Sally get something to eat in the kitchen, and maybe wash up before they did.

'No one's washed up for a week!' she shouted. 'We're running out of plates, dishes, cups and what have you. If your father was here he'd go mad. Alex Twentyman an easy lay? What a cattish thing to say,' she said turning to Fay. 'If you ask me she's just a very unhappy woman. I must try and do something about her.'

9

'Mrs Twentyman?'

'Yes.'

'It's Lorna Galbraith here. May I call you Alexandra?'

'Everyone calls me Alex.'

'Oh that's better, isn't it? I was given such a short name that I have a sort of suppressed envy of anyone with a long one. That's why I married George really. From Lorna Burke to Lorna Galbraith was a great improvement. Though if I had been in the Women's Movement then which of course I wasn't –it didn't exist – I should never have dreamt of changing my name. So I'd still be Lorna Burke.'

Lorna did go on, Alex thought, though not without amusement. She wondered what the children of the marriage would have been called. After all, they had their rights too, didn't they?

'Alex I don't know if you're the least bit interested, but one of our visiting professors needs a manuscript typed. Could you do it at home?'

Alex paused then, cautiously:

'I haven't a typewriter.'

'Couldn't you invest in one? It might be worth it if you liked doing that sort of thing.'

'What kind of manuscript?'

Really, thought Lorna, Alex wasn't being very co-operative or even keen-sounding for someone who needed work.

'Well it's sociology. He's a sociologist from Israel. A very nice man, Professor Itzhak Bar-Tur.'

'I don't know a thing about sociology.'

There, being uncooperative again. Sometimes Lorna wondered why she bothered. Here she was trying to help

Itzhak and trying to help Alex and wasting her precious time...

'You don't have to,' she said with some asperity. 'He's not asking you to help him write it, just type it. Would you like to see him and talk about it?'

'O.K.'

No, not interested at all. What a waste. You'd think Alex was doing *her* a favour.

'Right, I'll give him your number. By the way Alex, are you interested in joining our parents' committee? I'm the secretary and we need people just like you.'

'How like me?'

Oh my God, she was going to go on being obstructive. You'd think she'd be interested in the school. Keen to do something for it. Maybe she had one of her depressions, or her period perhaps.

'You know alert, active. We need representatives from every class. Do say yes.'

'What does it involve?'

'Just taking part in the school activities.' Lorna was aware of raising her voice. 'Organizing things. Attending meetings. Being part of the school. It's for your children too, Alex.'

'May I let you know about it?'

'Of course.'

Alex thought she probably would; but Lorna had a steamroller effect she rather resented. It made her procrastinate deliberately. She liked to think about things before being rushed into doing anything. Alex walked into a patch of sun that lay on the carpet. Mid October. Yes, just exactly a year since Harry had done a bunk. Now he wanted a divorce. She'd had a letter from her lawyer that morning which was why she'd felt blank and uncooperative with Lorna. What, after all, was the point of doing anything? Subconsciously Alex knew that she'd been hoping Harry would avoid this final step; that he'd get tired of clever Rosalind and want to come back to her and the kids. She'd still have him. She felt an awful yearning in her heart for familiar Harry and realized she was once again near tears.

She'd felt low for some days now and the letter had merely confirmed that there was nothing left to expect out of life. She'd woken in the middle of the night aware of the emptiness in the great bed; she'd put a hand out feeling Harry's place, trying to remember the smell of him, the feel of his long hard body. She'd even wished Toby had been there to cuddle. Just some comfort, companionship.

* * *

'I miss Harry so much. I really do. Everything I try and feel about him, against him, is hopeless. When I see him again I always want him. He looks different now you know, smarter, leaner; always trendy shirts and clothes. Rosalind said she'd put him on a diet because of this cholesterol business and I think Harry looks ten years younger. Why should she have him? Do you think she cared more about him to start him dieting? She looked so elegant too last Sunday; they almost looked the same age. By the way she's just 26. Maybe that's why she was so keen to get Harry, she's older than I thought. And they're having some important negotiations with a larger wine company to be taken over or merged. Very good anyway. Harry wants a divorce. Why should I give it to him?'

'Why not? You want to hold him down?'

One of Dr Dickson's rare interjections. She always called him *Dr* Dickson and not Dick – she doubted whether Emma had either, to his face. But Alex always thought of him as 'Dr' Dickson, her new father figure.

'Why should I let her have him so easily?'

'It's not her that matters, it's you. You're trying to convince yourself that Harry will come back. You're just prolonging the agony.'

'Harry might get tired of her. I do want him back. I still think of him as mine.'

'*Yours?*'

'Oh I know you think I'm too possessive. Yes, I do think of him as my husband, the kids' father. We took vows in church; we had a white wedding and received communion. It was very solemn; a bond; a contract. Now Harry just wants to tear it apart. You could never do that with any other business contract, why should you be able to in marriage? He took a vow and he's broken it. They want me to go on the parents' committee. There's this very bossy woman, Lorna Galbraith.

I don't want to be involved in the school. Why should I?'

'You just want to stay in your own little home and wait for Harry?'

'That's a silly thing to say; oh I know I'm not being realistic. And another thing, a man is coming round to see me about typing a manuscript. I think I'd get too lonely if I worked at home, yet I quite like the idea . . .'

She always did feel better after seeing Dr Dickson. All her contradictions seemed to cohere and synthesise after she left him. God knows what he really thought. He was more than usually talkative today. She sometimes felt he didn't really approve of her, or even like her. Did he think she was selfish? She swung into Bonnington Crescent and saw another car outside the gate and a huge man standing at the front door with a parcel under his arm. Oh God, why had she told him to come so soon? Why hadn't she thought about it a day or two? She didn't even have a typewriter.

She thought he was just about to go when she got out and walked up to the gate. He really was enormous, with curly black hair sprouting from a massive head and a lean dark face. Thin lips. Not really attractive at all . . . maybe she'd been half hoping.

'Mrs Twentyman?'

'Professor Bar-Tur? I'm sorry I'm late. Do come in.'

He stood aside for her, an awkward movement because he was so tall and the path up to the house small. He was huge, must be nearly seven feet, taller than Harry and he was well over six.

'Come in.'

'What an attractive house? So light.'

'Yes, we're lucky having the park opposite and a biggish garden at the back.'

'Charming.'

Professor Bar-Tur looked interestedly around.

'Come into the sitting room, please.'

She took off her coat feeling rather awkward; she felt tiny beside him.

'Would you leave your coat there?'

He wore a neat dark grey coat which made him look rather like a Rabbi. It was fastened up to the top button; no doubt he felt the cold. She was surprised to see underneath that he dressed well – a well-cut sports jacket in a mauvish tweed, tweed shirt and wool tie and trousers made from some sort of heavy bluish twill. His shirt collar buttoned at either side. Very American. When he spoke, he had a slight American accent. He walked ahead of her and sat clumsily down on the sofa, his parcel still in his hand. Such was his weight that he really sank on the sofa, and she thought if she sat next to him she'd slide on to him so she sat opposite.

'Can I give you some tea, coffee?'

'No thank you, Mrs Twentyman. I had some in college. Dr Galbraith said you might be interested . . .' he paused and thrust the long parcel out in front of him. Alex ran a hand through her hair.

'Well . . . the trouble is I haven't a typewriter.'

'Oh, she didn't mention that.'

She thought he looked rather annoyed and went on quickly.

'It was very kind of her and actually it is a good idea, to work at home, if I can find the work, that is, regularly you know. I'd be here for my children and able to plan my day.'

'Yes, it does sound a good idea.'

'I think maybe I can get a typewriter.'

'Oh fine. Shall I show you the script?'

He began to untie the string of the untidy parcel. She saw that his huge hands were awkward too – yet his fingers were long and elegant and the nails well kept, like Harry's. In fact he reminded her a little bit of Harry now she saw him closer. Of course Harry was much better looking, more elegant, but, yes, there was a likeness. Very hard to say how, because Harry's hair was always well groomed whereas Professor Bar-Tur's was like a tangled woolly rug. She felt she liked him that bit better for bearing a resemblance to Harry, and eagerly leaned over to see the manuscript.

Her heart sank. It was handwritten in tiny squiggly writing. There was masses of it, and figures . . . He watched her, anxiously sorting through the pages.

'It is long; but I am not in a great hurry. I want it well done, perfect, because it is to be published here and in America and each publisher must have a good script.'

'I see, yes, well . . . I have no idea how to charge for a thing like this.'

'Well you'll have to let me know, if you want to do it. I suppose it depends on whether you can get the typewriter?'

'Yes, it does.'

The professor stood up, the cushions on the sofa shooting up behind him.

'Could we leave it like that, Mrs Twentyman? What do you think? It's possible?'

'Yes, I think so. Yes, I'd like to do it.'

'Good.'

The professor walked to the door and looked round him again.

'It's a very charming house; nice atmosphere. Yes, I like it.' The way he talked you'd think he wanted to buy it. She saw him out and watched him squeeze himself into his tiny little car. He really was *huge.*

* * *

Alex approached Rosalind about the typewriter; she was more likely to get it from her, she thought, because Rosalind was always very anxious to please her, as though harbouring a suspicion of guilt about what she'd done. It would be nice to think so anyway. Also she didn't want to talk to Harry because of this business about the divorce. She hadn't said anything yet to the lawyer. She asked to be put straight through to Rosalind whose cool interrogative tones came soon after on the phone.

'Yes, Alex?'

It was 'Alex' now, had been for some time.

'Rosalind, it has been suggested to me I could work at home. You know I'd like that; be here when the children come.'

'What a good idea; doing what?'

'Well, typing; you know I've had these odd secretarial jobs which have been so unsatisfactory.'

'Yes, it sounds an excellent idea. Is that what you rang me about?'

'I need a typewriter.'

'Oh you haven't a typewriter?'

'No.'

'Oh. That's why you rang me, I suppose?'

'I wondered if you had one spare in the office?'

'No, we haven't. Can't you rent one?'

'I thought it would be nice to own one and I can't possibly afford it. I need a good strong electric typewriter. I already have a client with a manuscript.'

Her voice got more confident as she spoke. She resented this inquisitorial air of Rosalind, as though she were applying to her for a job.

'I'll talk to Harry. He's not here now. We may have some good news . . .'

Alex's mind flew to babies and she put a hand to her mouth to stifle a small cry of pain.

'. . . about the business. It may make Harry more amenable to the typewriter idea.'

Oh relief! Why did she care so much if they had a baby? Harry wanted to marry Rosalind, didn't he? For a moment, she realized, she's thought that that was the reason for asking for a divorce. She couldn't bear the idea of Harry's baby inside Rosalind.

* * *

To her astonished surprise Harry came that night, late and alone. The children were in bed but not asleep and he went up to see them. Alex felt nervous and confused and rushed around in Harry's wake like an anxious duckling after its mother. Harry smelt nice; he had a new after-shave lotion; his cheeks were blue with his beard. He had on a grey business suit, blue shirt and an expensive tie. His brown shoes looked hand-made or at least very expensive. Yes, Rosalind was improving his image all the time. Only from the distance that the year had brought could Alex see that this was so.

When he went into the sitting room, he looked around as if unaccustomed to the new furniture. Then he poured himself a drink as though he still lived there.

'Drink, Alex?'

'Thank you. Where's your keeper?'

'Oh Alex, I thought we'd got over that. I thought we were all quite friendly and civilized now.'

'She never lets you out of her sight though, does she?'

'Well, she has tonight. As a matter of fact she's a few doors away, seeing some friends who've just moved in.'

'Oh the Harrisons' place?'

'Yes, they're nice people. We had dinner there and I said I thought I'd wander over to see you.'

Harry's eyes glinted in a friendly way and he looked up at her.

'Cheers.'

She wished he lived here still; that this was his home; that they would go up to bed together, and the large bleak space beside her would be filled. It must have been the message in her eyes because he looked down into his drink.

'Ros says you want an expensive typewriter.'

'I want to work at home.'

'I think it's a good idea. Yes, I don't see why we shouldn't get you one on the firm.'

'Oh Harry, thank you . . .'

'It's the least I can do. Alex, you heard from Bleward?'

Bleward was Harry's lawyer.

'I heard from Mr Ross.'

Ross was her lawyer.

'I think we should make it neat, don't you? Tidy things up. Ros feels it.'

'Oh does she?'

'Now don't get funny again. I think Ros has behaved very well. Really very civilized.'

'Do you want children?'

'Oh good lord no. Ros even wants to be sterilized, but I thought that was going a bit too far. No she's quite decided.'

'And you don't mind?'

'Not at all. I have two, and children are largely for women anyway. I think the world would be depopulated if the choice were left to men.'

Certainly, if it were left to men to look after them, Alex thought.

'Don't you think it's funny she doesn't want children?'

Harry looked up at her and smiled. 'Poor Alex. Still the

pumpkin eater?'

Alex felt like crying. Her yearning for him, for a new baby and her old life was almost too strong.

'I felt cut off because I didn't have any more children. Incomplete. I still do.'

'Alex, I wish you'd get a boyfriend. Marry again. I really do. Believe me, I'm your best friend. I'm thinking of you.'

'Thinking of *me*?' Alex exploded. 'Do you know what you're saying, Harry, truthfully? Do you *ever* think of me? Do you know what it's like to be me? How the hell can I marry again, just like that?' Alex snapped her fingers in Harry's face and glared at him. 'I'm not a woman at a loose end. I have too much to do: children to care for, a house to clean and look after, shopping, meals to cook, endless washing with the kids needing clean clothes every day. When I have time, I'm typing to earn some money to eke out your meagre allowance, and when I'm not too exhausted in the evening I find time to watch television for an hour. Most nights I just crawl into bed only to find I can't sleep.

'What chance does all that give me to go out and find a man? My life is entirely centred on my home, on my surroundings. I have no office where I can meet people, no business lunches, no parties given practically every day by wine merchants . . . Oh no, Harry, when a marriage breaks and the kids are left with the woman, and they usually are, her life is certainly no barrel of fun. And the man? He seems to think he is the bachelor again, carefree. His first thought is to find a mate to take care of him, if he hadn't found one already, and he is usually successful. There are any number of women waiting, anxious to step into the breach. If I'd left you, how long do you think it would have taken you to find a new woman?'

Harry looked at the ceiling as though giving the matter serious attention; but the tap of his foot on the carpet showed he was getting impatient, even bored.

'A week, Harry? A month?'

'Oh come off it, Alex. You can always find someone to go to bed with. Any number of men . . .'

'I *cannot* find someone to go to bed with, Harry. For a woman like me it is not as easy as you think. Not . . .'

Alex gave vent to the tears which had been welling in her

throat, tears of frustration, but also because this was the first time she'd seen him alone for nearly a year. And now to have the husband she loved and wanted offering merely to be her friend. He was in love with somebody else and still she could not accept it.

'Oh Alex . . .' He came over to her and put a brotherly hand on her shoulder, squeezing it.

'Oh H . . . Harry. I wish . . .'

'You wish . . . I know what you wish. But it can't be, Alex. That is all over. And I'm a happier man. I'm sorry, but I am.'

Harry turned away and started to pace about the room.

'You can't tie your life down for other people. The kids seem happy and adjusted and if you had another bloke you'd soon forget about me. Honest, they're not as hard to find as you think. Try and move about a bit, Alex, please, circulate, for your own sake. I don't know that your working at home is so much of a good thing. You should get out and meet people.'

'I like to be home for the kids. I have to pick up Rachel. She's too small to travel on her own.'

'But with Toby . . .'

'I don't want them prowling on the streets. Harry, it's easy for you. All you did was move out, forsake your responsibilities. Why did you leave the children with me?'

Harry first looked surprised and then laughed.

'What would you have done if I had taken them?'

'But you didn't want them.'

'I knew you did. It's academic, Alex, and it really is over and done. If you won't let me have a divorce we'll wait, I'll get one after five years automatically. But it will make things less pleasant all round. Ros won't be nearly so co-operative, about the typewriter and that kind of thing.'

'Oh it's like that, is it? Blackmail?'

'My dear woman, it isn't blackmail! It's a question of human relationships, getting on. Oh damn, Ros said I shouldn't have come alone and she's right. You see Ros has been right all along to come with me. She knows how you feel. You really do feel bitter, don't you? I thought it would go, but it hasn't. She's a very astute young woman.'

Alex felt her wet, tear-stained face – the defeated, unwanted wife breaking down. The little woman just as Rosalind had expected. She didn't own Harry any more. Rosalind did. Now it came truly home to her; he no longer wanted or desired her, or even enjoyed her company apparently. She was a drag and a bore preventing him, with her tears and nagging, from leading the wholesome, exciting, successful life he craved, that he knew so well how to lead with that tawny exciting pony of a girl beside him.

'I'm sorry, Harry, I shouldn't have given in.'

'Oh that's O.K., Alex.'

False, utterly strange Harry again. What a remote man Harry had become. He turned round, his eyes glad that that nasty business was all over. 'I know it is hard for you but please, move about a bit. Get out more. Try and get married again. Despite what you've said, there are lots of men around. I'll see if I can think of someone.'

Alex thought how awful it was to have the man you loved and were still married to, offering you to someone else. Worse, offering to *find* you someone else, like some kind of pimp. She opened the door to let him out and watched him walk slowly, confidently along the street to be reunited with Rosalind. He didn't even turn back to wave. She was his past.

'Mum!'

'Toby, you should be in bed. Darling, it's late.'

The white figure, anxious, on the stairs, hair crumpled. Had he been listening?

'What did Dad want?'

She walked into the sitting room and he followed her.

'Have you been to sleep at all?'

'No. I wondered what Dad wanted. I hoped he'd want to come home. You look like you've been crying, Mum.'

The tears were there again. How unfair that this strong resolute little son, this companion, should grow up without his rightful father. Better that Harry had been killed on that plane. She took him on to her lap and snuggled her face in his hair.

'Toby, Daddy's never coming back. He wants to marry Rosalind.'

'Is that what he came to ask you?'

'Yes.'

'Oh Mum, don't let him.' Toby turned and she saw now that his face was creased by tears so that he looked as he had when he was small, like a baby crying. She pressed him against her bosom, wanting to cry too. She stroked his head and said, 'There, there,' just as Emma had the night Harry had not come home.

'Come on, darling. Let's go to bed.'

'But, Mum, can't you say to Dad . . .'

'Toby, I can't say anything to your father. He doesn't love me any more. He doesn't want to live here or be with us. He wants to live with Rosalind, start a new life with her.'

'Have children?'

'He says not. Oh darling,' she cuddled his head again, 'Daddy loves you very much, you and Rachel. He said tonight that he didn't want more children, he has two. He *does* love you! Anyway, you like Rosalind, don't you? You always have a good time with her?

'Yes, but it's not like you and Dad being together. I'd hoped he would get tired of her and come back here. Besides, Mum . . .'

'What?' she ruffled his hair.

'I think you're very lonely without Dad. I don't think it's fair on you.'

'I'm not as lonely as I was, and I have got you and Rachel. Besides, a lot of children are like you at the school, aren't they?' Parents not living together?'

'Uh uh.' Toby nodded thoughtfully.

'Well, you see, it's not so unusual. We just have to get used to it.'

'Well, I am used to it; but I still don't understand it. I love you and I love Dad. But why doesn't he love you?' Alex was close to breaking down again and gripped Toby fiercely.

'I can't answer that.'

'*You* wouldn't marry anyone else, would you, Mum?'

The waver in Toby's voice Alex understood. It was common for children to feel like this, even when their parent had been abandoned. They had to think they, the children, were the most important ones.

'Of course not, sweetheart, not yet, anyway.'

'Not *ever,* Mum.'

'Put it out of your mind, darling. Come on, let's go to bed.'

'Can I come in with you, Mum?'

Yes, she wanted his warm comforting body beside her, to help her through the night.

10

The annual meeting of the parents' association was sparsely attended as usual; just the staff and a few enthusiasts, maybe a fifth of the parents of children at the school.

'If they had to pay they'd all be here,' Lorna muttered angrily to Alex whom she had persuaded to come. 'See how their money was spent.'

'You mean there are so few people here because it's free?'

'Of course.'

'But I never went to the parents' association meetings of either of the children's private schools. Harry said seeing we paid so much we shouldn't need to. We could leave it to them.'

Lorna pondered the paradox presented to her by this unexpected reply, then turned to greet a tall woman whom Alex had seen before, the mother of a boy in Rachel's class on whom she had a crush, Franco. The mothers had smiled before, but never spoken.

'Carla,' Lorna cried. 'I haven't seen you for ages. Did you get to Italy in the summer?'

Carla smiled at Alex, again saying nothing, and sat down beside them in the fifth row. She had hair almost as fair as Alex and a long thin bone structure, good body and legs. Yet her face was lined and her eyes clouded; she did not look a happy woman.

'Yes, my parents paid. They wanted us to stay. I left Franco there for the holiday but I came back. I don't want to lose my patients.'

'Carla, do you know Alex Twentyman? You must. Franco and Rachel are in Mrs Richards' class.'

'Yes, we do but we haven't actually spoken,' Alex smiled and extended a hand. 'How do you do?'

Carla's careworn face was transformed by her smile, broad sensual lips like an Italian film star, and beautiful teeth. She had a soft Italian accented voice, husky like Sophia Loren.

'Franco is in love with Rachel. He talks of her the whole time.'

Alex laughed.

'I think it's mutual. She can't get over having boys in the class. She knew none before except Toby and Toby's friends.'

'Private schools! They're unnatural and breed homosexuality.' Lorna snorted.

'Lorna, I think that's single sex schools,' Alex said gently. 'I don't think it's anything to do with being private.'

'Most private schools are single sex schools.' Lorna replied 'That's why they're so degenerate.'

'Rachel was at a private school?' Carla raised thick untrimmed eyebrows.

But before Alex had time to reply the Head stood up to begin the meeting and introduce the items on the agenda. The committee was elected, Alex being proposed by Lorna and seconded by Carla, almost before she knew what was happening.

'I'm also on the committee,' Carla whispered conspiratorially.

Alex felt warmed by her smile. She'd known none of the mothers properly yet except Lorna, who had almost eaten her alive, and it was nearly half term. This she found so different from the private schools where the mothers seemed instinctively much more open and friendly. It was nothing to do with social class, Alex felt, but because somehow they all seemed in a hurry here and many more of them were working mothers. It was a factor which went along with being on your own, something she'd never noticed at the private schools where if the mothers were on their own they tended not to tell you. Or perhaps, Alex realized now, not being on her own she hadn't noticed, wrapped up in her own protectively cocooned world with her own husband and a comfortable well-kept home.

Lorna chaired the subsequent talk by the controversial junior government minister and Carla and Alex moved up and sat together, chatting afterwards and smoking. Carlo was a physiotherapist, it transpired, with her own small practice.

'It was so difficult to know what to do with Franco after school. I couldn't get away at a hospital and, besides, my husband was ill for a very long time and it was the only way I could nurse him and support us.'

'Oh I'm sorry.' Alex didn't want to ask the inevitable question but Carla supplied it.

'He died last year. He had cancer.'

'I'm terribly sorry.'

'He'd built up his own business and when he died everything was in such a mess – accountants and lawyers and the men from the Inland Revenue. He simply hadn't been able to cope for the two years he was ill . . .'

Carla bent her head as if recollecting the memory, the painful memory. It would have been like this for Alex if Harry had died.

'It takes years to get over it,' Carla said at last. 'I don't think I ever shall. Are you on your own?'

Alex resented the expression because, after all, it wasn't exactly true.

'The children do have a father,' she said defensively, 'we're separated.'

Carla shook her head.

'I can't understand why there are so many people separated. If they knew a loss like I had they'd stay together.'

Alex thought this unfair, but rather emotionally Italian.

'I don't think you can say that,' she said. 'It's like if you can't have children you feel so resentful about people who can and then leave or mistreat them. I think it is terrible and unfair even that a beloved husband dies and you are on your own, but it is also unfair when a man walks out, or a woman too I suppose, and leaves the other spouse grieving, not to speak of the children.'

'And that's how it was with you?'

'Yes, it's like a death for me too; only worse because he's there to remind me.'

'That you still love him?'

'Yes.'

Carla moved nearer as though to express sympathy. Alex felt the first rapport she'd had with a woman since Emma Drax, and that had worn pretty thin recently. Emma and Roger and Harry and Rosalind were a regular foursome, and Emma only ever popped in now as a kind of charity visit during the day when she happened to be passing. There was no rapport left there at all. Lorna she found too overpowering. The little she'd seen of Fay was slightly hostile and the rest were distant smiles or brief 'hellos' from people like Carla.

'Would you like to let Franco come to tea with Rachel one day?'

'I'd love it. I can fit a few more patients in that way.'

'And perhaps when you pick him up we can have an early meal together?'

'That would be nice.'

Carla's grateful smile seemed to indicate that she had very few friends too. Women on their own were very much on their own, Alex reflected; they had so much to do that an adequate social life was almost impossible.

Lorna bounced over, her arm through that of the junior government minister who of course was a close friend. The Galbraiths had the most well-connected friends in politics, the arts, medicine – to say nothing of writers, journalists and members of the academic profession. Lorna, this evening, had her large, errant bust constrained in a reasonably fitting bra and over it a blue wool dress made her look, for once, quite neat. Her beautiful hair was braided and her face betrayed her joy in her accomplishment.

'Alex, may I introduce Ben Farrow? Ben, Alex Twentyman and Carla I think you've met at our house once or twice.'

Mr Farrow smiled wearily and looked at his watch.

'D'ye do? Could we push off now Lorna, love? I have stacks of work.'

'Oh Ben, won't you come home for a bite?'

'Sorry, can't. Tomorrow I have to brief the Prime Minister at Question Time on education.'

'Oh. Terribly kind of you to come Ben, say goodbye to Tom.'

She took him over to the Headmaster, Tom Bridge, an enthusiastic capable man in his mid-thirties who had worked hard all his life to make state schools successful and was continually depressed by the war between the main political parties about education. Ben Farrow's speech had done nothing to make him feel any better, being full of hyperbole, invective against the Tory Party and class hatred – all the sort of things Tom tried to avoid in discussing education which he thought was mainly about the acquisition of knowledge.

Alex and Carla made for the door, Carla stopping to talk to people she knew, evidently a good many. By the door Fay was standing, a tall thin miserable-looking man behind her. She was obviously waiting to talk to Carla but nodded her head at Alex who stopped and smiled.

'Hello, did you enjoy the meeting?'

'Not much. This is the children's father, Jack. Alex I'm sorry I've forgotten your surname.'

'Twentyman,' Alex said politely shaking the tall man's hand. He looked nervous and said nothing. Fay always dragged Jack along to school meetings for the sake of the children, she said, to keep up appearances; in reality it was to try and make Jack feel guilty and thoroughly awful. Fay felt a continuing and ferocious hatred of her ex-husband who had not only left her but had married again, apparently happily, someone completely different from herself.

Jack's one ordeal was going to the flat which he did with the punctiliousness of a religious duty but without love. He felt he'd behaved badly and the thought tormented him; the faces of the children reproached him by their very indifference when he came to see them. Fay reproached him with her hate but he was used to that and more inured to it. He cared that the children should be indifferent to him even though he knew Fay did all she could to foster it.

Fay, who had resented having them so much, had poisoned their marriage with her fears and disgust at the sex act, so that she made him feel permanently abnormal and unclean, now was obsessed with caring about the children. She did love them; in her way she was a good mother, he knew that, but she was erratic, fond one moment, threatening the next so that the children had grown up uncertain and insecure. And she used their frequent bad behaviour to make Jack feel even worse. She'd have him in hospital with that depression again if she could. However, there was nothing he could do about it; his new wife, Joyce, wouldn't have the children at any price, not his. She wanted them cut out of her life and, with a small baby and another on the way, was busy producing her and Jack's own family to the complete exclusion of Fay's.

However, Jack felt a duty to his first family. He came sharp at seven every Thursday evening and sat staring at the children, not knowing how to converse with them. It got on Fay's nerves so much she could have screamed, the way he just sat there like a stuffed scarecrow. The kids would much rather have been watching TV or playing outside, if it was summer, on the piece of concrete littered with wood and broken glass so many miles down, it seemed, from their flat on the twentieth floor of the unpopular high-rise building. It made her dizzy even to look out and see if she could see them. It was all Jack's fault they were here at all.

Jack had 'pretended', in Fay's opinion, to have some sort of nervous breakdown after he left home – at that time they had a fairly decent flat in West Hampstead. He moved of course into his girlfriend's flat and from there into hospital and while he was away Fay had no one to turn to but the State. Now it sometimes seemed to own her completely and govern the way she breathed – family allowances, supplementary benefits, rent relief, goodness knows what.

Once a month Jack insisted on taking them to lunch at a cheap restaurant in Camden Town where all made a great effort to appear to be a normal family having a good time.

The ones who suffered most in all this charade were Jack and Fay. The children would much rather have got on with their lives despite the constant reminders from the welfare and others intent on doing good that they were deprived and somehow sub-standard. Amanda, the 8 year old in Rachel's class, still couldn't read and had to have special coaching in almost everything. Quentin who was 10 and in Toby's class, apart from being backward too, was aggressive and a perpetual threat to law and order. Only Ralph who had been the eldest when his parents split was in any way normal, and seemed to have any sort of future.

Carla and Fay were talking and making some kind of date, Fay in that quick nervous way she had, fumbling for things, dropping pencils, betraying with every movement her constant losing battle with the world. Jack just looked over Alex's head dispiritedly about him, not attempting to talk and Alex was keen now to get away.

'Alex dear, you're getting a typewriter I hear!'

Alex looked around startled. Why did Lorna have to inform the world of this fact, she wondered.

'Yes.'

'Oh that's splendid. And then you'll start on Itzhak's thesis?'

'Yes, I'm going through it with him to make sure I'll get it right.'

'Oh good. Isn't he a dear?'

'Very nice indeed. 'Bye Lorna.' Alex waved at her and all in general, escaping thankfully to her car.

Lorna gazed after her, her mouth pursed. Alex hadn't even said 'thank you'. She wasn't the least bit grateful for all she, Lorna, had done.

* * *

In the course of the next few weeks, October and November merging into the mellow changeable months of late autumn and early winter, Alex agreed to divorce Harry and as a present for being a good girl took delivery of a fine new electric typewriter. She also let the basement flat to a young American businessman, and she saw Itzhak Bar-Tur about once a week to go over points in his manuscript with which she was making slow progress.

'It isn't as though it's difficult to understand,' she assured him. 'It's interesting really, it's your writing!'

Itzhak gave an amused squirm which made the sofa wobble about dangerously.

'That I can do nothing about.'

'It's like a doctor's prescription writing, look.' Itzhak moved nearer to peer at the offending word and Alex was intensely aware of his proximity, his male presence, the pleasant alpine smell of soap or after-shave or whatever it was. Itzhak always looked and smelled terribly clean, almost fragrant in a quite uncissified way, like someone who paid a good deal of attention to his appearance. She used to try avoiding sitting next to him on the sofa, not only to prevent herself falling on top of him every time he moved, but also because this proximity was unnerving and tormenting to a woman who hadn't had sex for over a year, except for a brief interlude that summer.

Alex found that the sex problem waxed and waned; she wouldn't think about it for weeks and then she had it on her mind all the time. Everything took on a sexual connotation; she felt jealous and deprived and somehow permanently on heat. Then it would go and nothing would disturb her tranquillity for weeks. It seemed to be a sort of cyclical thing. She wondered how people did without sex all the time. Maybe that made it better; if you knew you weren't going to have it or couldn't get it you put it out of your mind. But she was always hoping; she couldn't imagine doing without sex forever.

It wasn't that she desired Itzhak; but she did like him and found his presence both welcoming and disturbing. Had he made any overtures she would have welcomed them, but he didn't. He never stayed long; it was strictly a business relationship and she'd give him a cup of black tea – he never drank anything else, no sugar, no lemon, just black – and go over the week's work with him, giving him what she'd done.

He paid her regularly and in cash and it was the one thing she felt good about as the preparations for the divorce seemed to race ahead – she was earning her own money. She was beginning to feel pride in standing on her own feet because otherwise she'd felt terribly reduced compared to, say, Rosalind who was not only earning money, a great deal of it by the sound of things, but had Harry as well and now this beautifully furnished (from what the children had told her) box in Putney. That was the only thing that did satisfy her, beginning to feel independent; the rest was awful. The children had started to quarrel incessantly – previously so docile, so even tempered, now they were forever at each other verbally, or physically if they got the chance. Most of the physical abuse seemed to come from Rachel, but then she would torment Toby so much that when he finally hit out he really hurt her.

Sometimes when she wanted to get on with the manuscript she felt so harassed she could have screamed. Her cleaner had gone long ago, of course, so she not only had to clean, cook, wash and shop but endure this constant bickering and slamming of doors that went with it. Half-term was almost unbearable until Harry complainingly agreed to have them in the office for one day, and apparently sent them to the pictures with the new secretary who had taken Rosalind's place now that she was a director.

Much was made of the fact by Harry that Alex seemed increasingly unable to cope with the children. Was she losing her grip, her cool? But why? She had a very pleasant life didn't she? She didn't *have* to work. She wanted to keep herself occupied. If it was that difficult she ought to stop and make do with the very generous allowance Harry gave her and the letting of the basement flat. When Harry, immaculate, appeared at the door to collect or deliver the children and Alex thought of the inequality of their situation, all the things she was doing for them and he wasn't, she felt belligerent and knew she looked it.

'But Alex, I never used to shop or cook or clean. I never did a thing for the kids.'

'But you were there Harry, you came home at night. You were here at the weekend, usually anyway. You don't know what it's like, how difficult they are, how lonely I am.'

Rosalind, who always came with Harry now since that evening because she wanted to keep her paws firmly on him, gave Alex her cool, slightly amazed appraising look.

'But Alex, I thought you liked kids.'

'Of course I like them!' Alex snapped.

'It's a good thing you didn't have any more then.'

Two blank disinterested faces looking politely at her. They really didn't comprehend. They had no idea what she was going through. And she knew the children were fine with their father, made a special effort to be nice when he was here. As soon as the door closed behind him a change went through the house like the advance ripple of a stormy easterly wind. A change that Harry, of course, was never around to feel.

And then just before Christmas, Emma Drax flew into the house one grey misty morning when Alex needed the light on to work and threw herself into a chair, coat and all, with a distraught expression.

'For God's sake what is it, Emma?'

'You mean you don't know?'

'Of course I don't.'

'No idea?'

'None at all.'

Emma had been studying her face and when, convinced at

last of Alex's innocence, she got dramatically to her feet, and swayed slightly either from a rush of blood to the head or from genuine distress.

'Harry has agreed to amalgamate the business with another company, to put it at its best. At its worst, to be taken over. And Roger is out on his arse. Thank you and goodbye.'

Alex got slowly to her feet and took a cigarette from the box on the mantelpiece. She was slowly trying to absorb information that she might have been expected to know already.

'I don't understand. Wasn't Roger a partner? Didn't he have some say in all this?'

'When Rosalind was made a director they rewrote the original partnership agreement between Harry and Roger. It's a limited company and Rosalind had insisted on being able to buy a third of the shares. I see it was carefully planned, now, months in advance and Roger's lawyer did warn him about it at the time, but Roger was too easy-going. He didn't believe it could happen and now it has. Harry and Rosalind together outvoted Roger. They've given him a very small silver handshake and told him goodbye. The brutality!'

She looked at Alex as though to say she considered it personally her fault. Alex was appalled. It seemed so unlike Harry.

She remembered the years of his friendship with Roger, going back to their apprenticeship in the firm of City wine merchants. It didn't seem possible Harry could do such a thing to an old friend.

'Of course it's not Harry, it's Rosalind,' Alex said when she spoke at last.

'But Harry's the . . .'

'Harry wouldn't do a thing like that. But sentiment would never be allowed to stand in Rosalind's way. She told me months ago things were getting better, but I never dreamed this was the sort of thing she meant. Which company?'

'Oh some big company in St James's. Harry and Rosalind are to join the board and take stock and goodwill of Twentyman and Drax. And Roger gets the rough equivalent of a year's salary. His lawyer is fighting it of course, but he doesn't seem hopeful. Roger was very silly and trusting when the company was formed.'

'I'm sure Rosalind wouldn't do anything that wasn't cast iron. Why is there no place for Roger?'

Emma shrugged and threw herself into the chair again, hands deep in the pockets of her heavy tweed coat.

'They don't need him. If you ask me I don't think they think he's any good and you know what? I agree with them. Roger made all the bad decisions that have been taken, like the heavy investment in claret which started the trouble in the first place. I know it was all Roger's fault.'

'Harry always felt Roger had the better palate,' Alex said offering a crumb of comfort.

'He was right, but Roger has no business sense. God knows what will become of him now. The wine trade is like death with the new increase in wine tax – 5p on a bottle. We might even have to take Portia away from the convent.'

Alex thought if this was the worst that happened, the Draxes would be lucky and she told Emma so.

'I don't agree. I think your children have deteriorated terribly since they've been at the Princess Maud.'

Alex, all bristles: 'What do you mean by that?'

'They've got noisy, aggressive, bad mannered, bad tempered. You can hardly recognize them.'

'That's nothing to do with the school. That's because Harry left home. Left me on my own.'

'But I didn't notice it before this term dear. Harry left home eighteen months ago.'

'It's a slow process of deterioration.'

'Which that school speeded up. Alex, you've got to agree.'

Alex wandered over to the window and stared out into her beloved garden, partly obscured in the morning mist, full of dead leaves and damp twigs, badly neglected by her this hot summer. She could only garden when she was tranquil and that was an emotion long lost to her.

'I don't necessarily agree. I just don't know. There are a lot of nice kids and nice people at the school. Just because it's free doesn't mean that the children should be unruly.'

'Nonsense. *Anything* free is disastrous. People don't appreciate it. Look at the new council flats that have to be pulled down because they're so vandalised. Look at the state of the health service, the abuse of social security. I believe in private medicine, private schools and a private life. I don't want others to suffer, but I don't want to be dragged down to their level. You know what? I'm going to try and get a job. Oh I know I've never done anything with my degree, but I do have one and I'm going to have a bloody good try.'

Looking at her, little mouth pursed in determination, Alex thought Emma had every chance of succeeding. She was one of those people who thrived on disaster. Alex felt that she, on the other hand, just went down under it. She felt embattled and embittered by the year she'd spent, defeminised and dehumanised, resentful and full of real or imaginary grievances.

She thought she was a less nice person than she had been, less pleasant and less attractive. And it was all because she'd only wanted what a lot of women did, expected, the majority maybe – to stay well and truly and, if possible happily, married to the same man all her life.

11

Half-way through the spring term the children started swimming lessons again at the Swiss Cottage baths. Twice a week Alex sat in the gallery looking down into the clear waters of the Belsize Pool where Rachel still struggled in the ducklings' class, but Toby was an advanced improver. Occasionally they'd look up at her for an encouraging smile and she'd sit there, with her head leaning over the balcony, ready to give it.

This was a new season and looking down on the first day she recognized the brown body of Franco, Rachel's boyfriend, frisking alongside her. She felt at the same time a stab of guilt. She had never, after all, invited him to tea. She was forever making excuses because she was nearly always tired or preoccupied or both.

Itzhak's thesis was nearly finished. He was going back to Israel and she would miss him, even though their relationship had never progressed beyond the merely friendly. She knew nothing about Itzhak's private life and he never enquired about hers. He was a very strange man, she felt, very academic.

Nor had she seen much of Lorna, though she saw more of her than anyone because Lorna rather intruded herself upon you whether you wanted to see her or not. She had roped Alex in to helping to run the Christmas party for the parents' association.

Alex's gaze slid along the gallery, past the overhanging heads of proud mothers and some proud fathers, and yes there was a long curtain of blonde hair hanging down towards the water, a wrapt anxious face which she recognized as Carla Nugent, Franco's mother. She left her seat and walked round to Carla touching her on the shoulder.

'Hello!'

'Why! Ah! Mrs Twentyman.'

'Alex.'

'Of course. I'd temporarily forgotten your name.'

'We didn't meet after all, and you weren't at the parents' party?'

Carla tossed back her thick honey-coloured hair, an abject expression on her face.

'I . . . sometimes feel I just can't cope. I mean I can do my job and that's about all. I hardly ever go to the school these days. I've had a lot of Ted's business things still to clear up, but I think it is over now. Franco has been very withdrawn as a result and Mrs Richards talked to me only yesterday about him. She said I don't spend enough time with him.'

'Come back for tea now. Can you?'

'Why? Why not?'

'Good.'

Alex was excited at the thought of having a friend to tea. She still had some of Harry's wine in the cellar, not much, and as it was Thursday and late night opening at Sainsbury's she could get something decent to eat on the way home.

It was a jolly party. Carla went ahead with the children and Alex stopped off at Sainsbury's and bought some minced beef so that the children could have beefburgers, and veal escalope for herself and Carla.

When she got home the house was echoing to laughter instead of quarrels and Alex felt both guilty and ashamed that she hadn't recognized the source of her children's bad behaviour: she didn't entertain enough for them, and was always yelling at them to shut the door or shut up because she was working. She'd become very interested in sociology on account of Itzhak's book and was thinking of starting a course at the evening institute – social movement of population, which was Itzhak's subject. It was fascinating to find out why people had gone where they had and the consequences for society.

She and Carla chatted in the kitchen, Carla proving adept at peeling onions and making real tomato sauce.

'Next you come to me and I do you a lovely spaghetti. You like pasta?'

'I love it, we never make it though. Harry says I should watch my weight. It's true I have put on a few pounds since

I settled down to work at home. Before that I lost it.'

'*He* says. Does he still tell you what to do?'

Alex laughed awkwardly. 'Well he takes an interest. I think what he really wants me to do is find a new man and if I get fat I won't. I'm still on his conscience. Besides he and his girl friend are awfully slim and diet-conscious for health reasons as well as vanity.'

'You like her?'

'Well we just about get on.' Alex tossed the beefburgers into the fat. 'I think I'm used to her more than anything. I do think she's good for Harry, which may seem a funny thing to say, but then I think I've finally accepted they're getting married now and that's it.'

'Oh you are divorced?'

'Nearly. They plan to get married at Easter.'

'Not much time.'

'For what? I don't want to stop it. I just want to get it over. Then I don't have any claim on him at all. Now I still half hope he'll change his mind.'

'Still?'

'Yes. Still. There, that's that. Lashings of chips and presto!'

Alex took the plates to the kitchen table and called the children. For the next half hour Carla saw to the children while she prepared the dining room for herself and Carla. She'd got a good bottle of wine from the cellar as soon as she came home and decanted it, hoping it would reach room temperature by the time they ate. She hadn't forgotten her wine training.

She set the table nicely in the dining room thinking what a long time it was since she had eaten there; she mostly ate either in the kitchen or off a small table in front of the telly. She and Harry had always had a semi-formal dinner in the dinning room, every night.

She lit a candle and when Carla saw the table and the care Alex had taken and then the food she was first surprised and then touched.

'But this is very special!'

'I felt like doing something different.'

'Are we celebrating something?'

'No. Well, yes, I've nearly finished the book I've been typing. It took me four months and has given me a new interest.'

'The author?'

'No,' Alex laughed, thinking how she'd at first rather hoped the nice-smelling, clean Itzhak would take an interest. All that had passed long ago because he never had. 'No. Sociology.'

'Ah, sociology.'

'I hope next year to register for a degree with the Open University.'

'What a marvellous idea.'

'It's a goal and you don't have to have any fantastic qualifications which I haven't got, such as you need to get into a university.'

'They say it's hard work.'

'Oh it's a slog. I think I'll enjoy it. Getting up early to watch the TV programmes. It will also fill the winter evenings.'

'Nothing else fills the winter evenings?'

Alex looked at Carla's face, correctly interpreting the unspoken enquiry.

'No. No men.'

'I can't understand it. You're such a pretty woman. Or do you put them off?'

'Maybe. I don't meet them on the whole. I rather like the professor, but nothing's happened there and now he's going home. No there's no one.'

'No sex?'

Alex didn't reply at first, feeling shy. She'd never discussed sex with anyone, any other woman. Emma Drax had always tried to draw her out and had never succeeded. Alex felt that sex was a very intimate, personal thing between you and your husband or whoever.

But things were very different now from what they had been eighteen months ago; she no longer had a husband or a lover or a sex-life. She was no longer that self contained, maybe self absorbed, rather remote lady who ran her life along well-oiled parallel lines. She was now one of life's casualties – or rather, she preferred to think, a fighter in the midst of battle, for she had not admitted defeat.

Carla seemed aware of her inner struggle because, from looking keenly at Alex, she turned her head away.

'Sorry if I'm being personal.'

'No. It's just that I never talked about sex before with anyone except Harry. I know a lot of women do; but I never found the need.'

'Most women talk about nothing else,' Carla said laughing, 'you must have been *very* unusual.'

'To answer your question I don't have a normal sex life,' Alex said slowly. 'I mean I try and put the whole thing out of my mind. Mostly I succeed. It's the only thing to do, like people in prison. Though I do regard it as completely unnatural. Harry and I had a very good sex life – not good enough apparently, for him.'

She pressed her lips together grimly.

'You consider your life a kind of prison?'

Alex pushed away her empty plate and gazed at Carla. Carla had the sort of uninquisitive impersonal approach of a doctor. Alex supposed it came from her relationship to the medical profession; there was something very clinical and detached about Carla that made it all right to have this kind of conversation with her.

'You know, I suppose I do. I never thought about it like that. My analyst says I am still living in the past; never knew how to adapt to new circumstances.'

'Your analyst! That must cost.'

'I don't see him so much now, maybe once a month. He helped a lot at first over Harry. I was so full of resentment, so sure Harry was wrong. Now I'm not so sure.'

'But why?'

'Well you get a better look at yourself when you're alone. I mean I think Harry was very wrong to behave the way he did and in the manner he did and all that; but I can see that there was something about me that made living with me difficult. I was overwhelmingly houseproud, terribly domesticated. I think it must have made me rather dull.'

There was a ring at the front door and Alex looked at her watch. Surely Harry . . .

But it was Milton the American from downstairs. Milt he called himself. She hardly ever saw him; his rent was paid in advance to the agency and apart from that he seemed entirely self-sufficient. He was also away a great deal.

'Oh Milton, come in. Is there something wrong?'

'I just came to see if your lights were on. I appear to have lost power.'

Milt was a good looking, clean limbed archetypal American young male of average height. She knew he was in the oil business but nothing else about him. They mostly exchanged greetings though once she had asked him for a drink and he had returned the invitation around Christmas time.

'Oh dear. I don't know a thing about fuses.'

'Well I do if you have some wire and I could borrow a torch.'

'Of course. Come and have a drink. We hardly ever see each other do we? This is Carla Nugent, the mother of a friend of Rachel's from school. You can hear the din upstairs.'

Carla inclined her head and Milt bowed and shook her hand.

'Sit down, Milt, and keep Carla company while I look for a torch and fuse wire.'

The fuse wire was among a tangled mess of string and bits of rope in one of the kitchen drawers. The torch she couldn't find and went upstairs to ask Toby. As usual it was in action as a military searchlight – Toby had his complete arsenal out to the delight of Franco. Rachel was rather reluctantly cast, once again, in the passive role of nurse while Toby and Franco were front line commandos.

'But, Mum, it's a searchlight.'

'I must have it, darling. Besides I told you not to use it in case the battery ran out when we needed it, like now.'

Alex grasped it firmly and went down the stairs into the dining room to where Carla and Milt were engaged in the sort of animated conversation that she hadn't expected. Carla was smiling and looking languorous and sexy and Milt was leaning towards her, his thin profile somehow active and urgent.

Yes, Carla was very sexy, Alex decided, looking at them for a moment through the glass partition. She found her attractive, but not in a sexual sense. She thought she was intriguing and, yes, it was the emanation of sex, someone infinitely alluring. Now as Carla sat on the chair her long legs were crossed sideways so as to expose the best part of them almost to the thigh, a sight not lost on Milt. Her head was tossed back, her lips parted and her eyes were alight with laughter, while the thick blonde hair swayed sideways with every movement she made. The thin cigarette between her long capable fingers looked sexy too. She had a lean strong muscular body with a very small bosom and she wore a skirt and a shirt with most of the top buttons undone.

Alex felt she was interrupting something when she went in and Milt stopped talking and awkwardly rose to his feet.

'I was just telling Carla about visiting the new oil rig. It is quite a spectacle.'

Alex thought you could say anything as a prelude to love, even a description of a visit to an oil rig could be made to sound romantic. He took the proffered torch and fuse wire reluctantly, Alex could see.

'Well thanks, Alex. I'll see what I can do.'

'Let me know if you need any help.'

'Nice talking to you, Carla.'

''Bye.'

Carla said nothing but inclined her head again, an enticing inviting smile on her lips which subtly changed into a merely pleasant expression when Alex sat down again.

'What a fascinating young man. How long has he lived here?'

'Oh, about six months. You find him fascinating?'

'Don't you?'

'Not at all. I think he's a rather nice, ordinary, 100 per cent American boy.'

'And there's never been anything between you?'

'Of course not. Besides he's about six years younger than I am. He's only 26.'

'So, is that a lot?'

'Carla, I'm just not interested and he's not either. But I could see he took to you. I think you were flirting with him.'

Carla laughed her sexy laugh and lit another cigarette.

'Oh you saw that, did you? But then I am *twelve* years older than him.'

'You're *never* 38!'

'I am! You see my face is lined if you get near; but I have a good body and I keep it well on account of my job. No, I like young men; they excite me.'

Alex was busily digesting this surprising information that Carla obviously had an active sex life.

'You do have then . . .'

'Affairs? Of course. I can't do without sex. Never could. Oh don't look shocked.'

'I'm not shocked,' indignantly, from the newly enlightened Alex.

'. . . surprised then; but that's why I asked about you. I knew we should get down to sex sooner or later. I'm not ashamed of it; it's natural after all. When Ted was very ill it was the thing that kept me going. Just casual sex so that I could concentrate on him without being bitter and warped. Does it shock you now, that I can be like that with a sick husband?'

'A bit,' Alex admitted, reluctantly. 'But I never judge . . . '

'It was quite outside my feeling for Ted. I knew he was dying. You know some very sick people go into themselves and the relationship changes. From being wife and mistress I became a wife and nurse. Your life centres round pills and bedpans, treatments, visits to hospital. I had to have something to remind me that life could still be normal in order to keep my sanity when this young man in his thirties was wasting away.'

'And you never get involved?'

'Oh sometimes, but not recently. Some of the men are my patients, no nothing indiscreet *there* of course – very professional at work, but if they ask me out privately . . . that's a different matter. I can do what I like with my private life. No, to me sex is something natural and normal, not a big mystery. That's why I don't understand about you, Alex.'

Alex began not to understand about herself either. Of course she didn't have men patients, which must have been a big help, but was there something wrong with her?

'If I had a man like Milt living in the same house, why I wouldn't hold back for a moment. But . . .' Carla frowned and looked at the candle flickering now in the sconce, 'just now I have a difficult decision. Something I can't decide.'

'Let's go into the sitting room and I'll get coffee.'

'No, I can't stay too late. Look I'd like to tell you now. You might help me. Whereas I have a lot of boyfriends I have no close women friends. I don't really know what to do. This evening has made us close, yes? I feel I can talk to you.'

'Then tell me.'

Alex joined her hands on the table and rested her chin on them. She felt flattered but anxious at the same time. What sort of confidence was she about to hear?

'Well I have a client, a man, who has a friend who is opening a new massage parlour in Soho. He wants me to work for him.'

'A massage parlour?'

'You know. Massage, yes, and everything else. I like casual sex, but I don't know I want it that casual.'

Alex was absolutely shocked. If Carla meant what she thought she meant, she could never conceive of anyone even considering such a thing.

'You couldn't do it, could you?'

'I . . .'

'I've shocked you. You see I'm very used to the human body. I pummel it and knead it every day. It doesn't really shock me; but to give them the sexual thrills they're looking for or whatever as a *job* . . . to be paid for it. That's why I hesitate.'

'But aren't you satisfied with your normal job?'

'Oh very happy, very satisfied, but Alex it doesn't *pay*. I never have enough money. I am always worried about it – the mortgage, repairs on the car, so on and so on. I would like to send Franco to boarding school, I can't. I'd thought about the job just to get a little relief from financial worry. The pay is fantastic and it is mostly tax free, in tips, and just for jerking them off or some little special thing they like. I mean it's not prostitution. They call it "relief from tension".'

'It sounds much harder work!' Alex laughed uneasily. She was trying to think if she would ever need money badly enough to consider such a thing.

'Oh it will mostly be massage, sauna, you know. But . . . I ask myself is it the first step down? What would my son say if he knew?'

'He might be grateful to a mother who loved him enough to do such work for him. I don't know.'

Alex surprised herself by what she said and felt herself blushing.

'Alex, what a sweet thing to say. You are not a professional virgin after all.'

'Of course I'm not a virgin!'

'Oh I don't mean a technical virgin. But you do put that air around, you know. *Noli me tangere.* Do not touch me. Maybe it put the professor off. Maybe it's why you don't like to talk about sex.'

Alex was silent while she absorbed what Carla was saying. She'd said Itzhak had never made any gesture, but neither had she. Maybe he thought she was cold and frigid and hadn't dared try.

'You think I should do it? Only a few hours, two days a week. And I'd earn as much as I make all week with my practice working hard, eight to ten hours a day.'

'Please don't ask my advice. I simply can't advise on anything as outside my experience as this. I can only say if you don't feel too repelled you can only try it.'

'Still I'm scared.'

Franco burst into the room, fully dressed in Action Man kit.

'Mama. He has *so* many toys. Come and see.'

Carla got up and took his hand, smiling at Alex.

'More toys too, you see.'

* * *

Alex wasn't surprised when the next day Milt came up to return the torch and fuse wire and started to talk about Carla. He wanted to know who she was exactly, what she did and where she lived. Most of all, what about her husband?

'He's dead. He died a year or two ago of cancer.'

'He was an Englishman?'

'Yes. She's more or less adopted England now and doesn't want to go home.'

'Do you think she'd go out with me?'

'Why don't you ring and find out? I'll give you her number.'

Milt didn't want to talk to her, only find out about Carla. As soon as he got the phone number he gave a yelp of excitement and ran down the back stairs to the entrance to his flat.

Alex couldn't decide whether she was jealous of Carla or what. Why didn't she attract men just like that? She knew she was pretty, men turned their heads to look at her still. *Noli me tangere,* Carla had said. Don't touch. This space is reserved for Harry and of all the men in the world he is the one who least wants to touch it.

Later that week Itzhak came to collect the final pages of the manuscript. Alex had spent all afternoon going over it and making sure there were no mistakes.

'You've done an excellent job, Mrs Twentyman.'

'It's a pleasure, Professor.'

Yes, after all this time, 'Professor' and 'Mrs Twentyman'.

'I can't thank you enough for your care.'

'Tea?'

'As usual? Yes please. Of course how can we let this solemn occasion pass without the customary libation?'

Itzhak smiled at Alex and she smiled back. It was the first relaxed warm smile she'd seen him give her, as though some tension had gone out of the relationship. She felt herself responding and something inside her melting – was the ice breaking at last?

'I could open a bottle of wine and we could really celebrate. After all it's the first manuscript I've ever typed.'

'Oh but I can go out . . .'

'No, no my husband was, is rather, a wine merchant.'

Alex aware of growing excitement flew out and down to the cellar. She placed the bottle in a basket and drew the cork in front of Itzhak's eyes – she always thought of him as Itzhak, no matter what she called him.

'I see you know a lot about wine.'

'Only how to serve it. My husband was very fussy and it's become ingrained.'

She showed him the cork, poured out a drop for herself, drank it and nodded.

'Good.'

'I'm impressed. Cheers, Mrs Twentyman.'

'Cheers, Professor.'

They toasted each other, their eyes meeting and then they laughed as though in mutual understanding that the situation was ridiculous.

'Itzhak,' he said. 'You must call me Itzhak.'

'And I'm Alex.'

'Alex? It is a man's name?' Itzhak frowned.

'Alexandra.'

'Ah, that is pretty. I shall call you Alexandra. It's a beautiful name. ALEXANDRA.' Nursing the syllables with his tongue.

He motioned her to sit on the sofa and then sank down beside her. The cushions tilted and, as she knew she would, she slid towards him, her glass tilting too.

'Oops.' She righted herself and saw that she had slopped

some wine on her jeans.

'I'm sorry.'

'That's all right. They're going to the launderette tomorrow. Well, Itzhak, I shall miss you and the manuscript. Let me know what happens. Keep in touch when you've gone.'

She said this very lightly because she really was sorry now that he was going; that they'd wasted all these months just in being polite.

'I am not going,' Itzhak said. 'Didn't I tell you? I thought I told you.'

He looked at her with a genuine air of puzzlement and she felt her heart lurch and start to race. She was being quite absurd.

'You're *not* going back to Israel?'

'No, I am staying on at least for another year, maybe two. You see I want to go on with my researches and all the material is here. Besides . . . ' he gave a heavy sigh and shrugged his shoulders, 'I don't really want to return to Israel or go back to the States. I like London. I'd like to settle here if the opportunity arose. Maybe Professor of Demography at some new university? It's an idea.'

Alex knew she mustn't be silly and excited. This had nothing to do with her; he wasn't doing it for her or with her in mind and, for God's sake, she was behaving like a small girl. He was hardly looking at her, just twisting his glass and studying the full rich colour of the wine.

'So. I hope one day you will do some more work for me.'

He drank his wine and got up suddenly, shooting her up on the cushions.

'I must go.'

'But there is all this wine left.'

'I'm sure you can drink it.'

Alex felt a kind of desperation that he was about to go; no more contact, really. No excuse to phone him. Nothing more for her to type just now. She was letting him go and she knew she would regret it if she didn't even try – he could always refuse. Say no, and then she would know he wasn't at all interested.

'Itzhak, I've some cold beef in the fridge. Won't you stay and have a bite? Finish the wine? That's if you've nothing . . .'

She was smiling in a bright detached sort of way as though to say that she didn't really care if he stayed or not. It was just that there was this beef.

Itzhak looked at first startled; then thoughtful, as though he was considering some obscure point to do with the movement of populations.

'Why, there is no reason I shouldn't stay if it is no trouble. Very kind of you, Alexandra. Are you sure?'

'Oh yes I'm sure. Sure.'

It was silly, it was girlish, it was ridiculous. It would lead to nothing and she was stupid to hope.

But she was so glad Itzhak was staying, that the ice that locked her, that bound her to Harry was beginning to thaw.

12

Carla changed into her new uniform and looked at the effect in the mirror. It was ridiculous. For the first time she despised herself. She was doing it for money; for sordid gain. She was a well qualified physiotherapist, a member of the Royal College of Physiotherapists and she was using her skills corruptly.

She wore a silly two-piece outfit that hid nothing, that was meant to be easily undone or opened or felt into. She knew that her legs would look fantastic emerging from the orange silk briefs; even her small bosom wouldn't look too bad under the tight wrap-round blouse that left her midriff bare.

She'd started early. It was her first day. They were still sweeping the streets of Soho, the stalls were empty and most of the shops only just open. She'd dropped Franco off at school and driven to Soho Square where she'd found a meter. If she could, she'd pop out and feed it, if not she could now afford to pay a fine with the money she would be getting.

Franco's mother. What would he think? What would Mrs Richards think if she knew what Franco's mother was doing, and the Head?

There was a knock on the door and the friendly voice of the manager called softly.

'Think you've got a client dear.'

She opened the door and gazed at him, swallowing hard. He was a nice business-like young man, not at all hard looking or corrupt as you'd expect. In fact you would have thought he led a singularly virtuous life.

'Stage fright? Don't be nervous, dear. All the girls go through this, but they quickly get used to it. I never knew one who didn't. It's not as though you've got to lie back and open your legs for the first time to some complete stranger. We have a much better class of client here. Our prices are high and our girls are the best. There, I'll introduce you and leave you with him. Some like you to help them off with their clothes, some don't. You'll soon see. This is one of our regular clients.'

The manager strode briskly in front of her and knocked discreetly at one of the cubicles, not pausing for an answer as he opened it.

'Ah, good morning sir. This is Miss Carlotta who has just joined us. I'm sure you will find she is very anxious to please you, sir. She is very well qualified.'

Carla closed her eyes and tried to pretend this was a normal patient coming for physiotherapy. He looked quite nice; fleshy, about 50, heavy-lidded eyes. He was sitting on the sofa in the pleasant shaded cubicle apparently drinking Scotch. He looked up at her and then down her legs and nodded.

'Come and sit here, darling.'

The manager shut the door, winking encouragingly at Carla. She sat on the hard sofa next to the man and he immediately put a hand on her leg. He'd bought her for an hour, but the manager had made it quite clear that the girls needn't agree to intercourse if they didn't feel like it. First and foremost they were masseuses.

Carla smiled politely at her client and got up. She fixed the towels on the business-like couch and turned round.

'Are we ready?'

The man with the hooded eyes looked at her. He couldn't quite make this one out. He got up and started taking off his clothes, pausing every few moments for a drink. His breath smelt heavily of whisky, but Carla noticed that his body was clean and he was not unpleasant, only vastly overweight. He finished his drink and lay on the couch face down; gave a deep sigh as he rested his head on his hands. After his first invitation he hadn't said a word.

'Don't you like the sauna first, sir?'

'It's bad for my heart. I got a bad heart.'

'You shouldn't be drinking whisky at nine in the morning in that case.'

'Who said so?'

'I'm sure your doctor said so.'

She covered his upper half with warm towels and began

gently to rub the backs of his legs.

'I've had two heart attacks already. I'm only 50. It's the life I lead. It's killing.'

She felt his body relax to her firm, professional touch.

'Say, you do it good. You professional?'

'Sort of.'

'I take a massage twice a week and then I go home to bed. I work nights.'

Carla had been told not to ask questions, however curious. The client would always provide the answers if he needed to. Mostly they just wanted to ruminate.

Carla went about her task until at last she heard him gently snore. First the legs then the toes, the overweight fleshy bottom covered with little black hairs, the broad hairy back, the shoulders. Really it wasn't too bad.

'Turn over,' she said gently. He stopped snoring and looked at her.

'This is the bit I like,' he said.

He already had an erection when she turned him over. He'd been lying there thinking about it. It was what he'd come for; poor tired man who worked all night and had a bad heart. He looked at his throbbing erect penis and he looked at her slyly, nodding towards it. She gingerly cupped her hand round it but he shook his head; she could see his pulse beating quickly in his neck.

'Take it in your mouth, darling.'

* * *

For the first week Carla felt she couldn't stand it. She felt debased and mortified; she felt used, a passive object, her hands and her mouth perpetually busy pleasing men she would never normally meet in her social life. They all seemed to come from the fringes of the underworld, or very high-powered, slightly dubious business activities. Most of them were well dressed and not offensive, but some of them smelt bad and these were the ones she hated.

Her hands felt rotten and her mouth felt putrid, but the worst thing was that she didn't feel like making love normally. She'd look at Milt's body and feel tired and sick; but she still made an effort because she didn't want him to know.

It was unfortunate that Milt's interest coincided with her decision to work in the masage parlour. She liked him and she welcomed him as a lover and took him immediately into her bed. But it wasn't only that; the excitement of an experienced older woman, a young energetic man. They had a lot in common. They liked dancing, Italian food and the cinema. When they could they'd spend the evening in bed eating pasta and watching the TV. She soon realized that Milt was her most serious affair since Ted had died; but she tried to compartmentalize her life with him and her work in Soho. It wasn't easy.

The second week was a bit better because custom had rationalized her disgust. She'd also talked to many of the other girls and found they were mostly single mothers like her, some unmarried, who were using the only thing they had to make the kind of money they wanted. Not just some money, because you could do that working in a restaurant or an office; not money that merely eked out an existence, took you half way towards the social security office; but real money. Those who did it full time were quite wealthy providing they escaped the clutches of the Inland Revenue; maintaining an unostentatious lifestyle was not always easy to people who had been poor.

The girls were a cheerful ordinary lot; women like her. Mostly young, younger than her, pretty, well spoken. They lived in all different parts of London in nice little flats, many of them had houses. They drove cars and some of them sent their children to private schools.

Some even enjoyed the life and liked their customers.

'You get fond of them, know their little ways.'

'But doesn't it affect your sex life?'

'Oh I haven't had a boyfriend for years. I just don't have that kind of inclination any more.'

But most of them had boyfriends, one or two even had husbands. One had five children. Carla watched them come briskly to the back door by the side of the restaurant, smart women in bright raincoats, high boots, fur coats. Then in the dressing room they quickly stripped, dressed in the fancy outfit, put on more make-up, a touch of perfume and, with a bright professional smile, they were gone to their duties.

Most agreed it was a cut above ordinary prostitution and few of the men wanted straight ordinary intercourse in the missionary position.

Carla began to be quite friendly with one or two of the girls. But somehow she was still disgusted with herself; not with them; she knew their motives and respected them. But did she want money that badly, really? Would she ever get used to what she was doing? Would she ever be as objective as she was about being a physiotherapist?

Even after a month Carla thought the answer was no.

* * *

'Something worries her,' Milt confided in Alex. 'There's something about her I can't understand. Do you know what it is?'

Alex who hadn't seen Carla since that night at her house didn't know, but she could guess. Milt's dating Carla had coincided with what Alex assumed was her decision to work part-time at the massage parlour.

Milt was crazy about Carla; he was talking about marriage and goodness knows what from the very first date. He didn't care about the difference in their age or anything. He said it was love at first sight and Alex believed him.

'She's tired all the time. I hope she's not ill. Alex could you try and find out?'

'I don't know her very well, really.'

'Please, Alex.'

'O.K. I'll phone her tomorrow.'

Alex was reluctant to interfere in the private life of two people she hardly knew. But she was curious about Carla; she couldn't help it. When she rang, Carla sounded guarded on the phone but said that 'yes' Franco could come to tea.

'I'll pick him up from school and bring him home afterwards.'

'Oh that would be nice. My car's being serviced.'

Alex thought at first when she brought Franco back the next day that Carla wasn't going to ask her in. She peeped through the door and made it only wide enough for a small child to come through.

'Thank you very much, Alex.'

'That's all right. How're things?'

'Fine. I do expect a patient any moment . . .'

She looked at Alex, seeing the expression on her face, knowing she was being rude.

'Come in for a quick drink.'

'Thanks.'

Yes, Carla did look tired, Alex thought, studying her surreptitiously as she prepared the drinks. It was the first time Alex had been to the house and its size and location surprised her. The mortgage and upkeep must have been enormous, and to one side Carla had had a separate annexe built for her practice. The sitting room was well and expensively furnished, even luxurious. The sideboard was stacked with bottles. Not just any old whisky, but malt whisky. Not any brand of sherry but the best, and not just amontillado but fino, manzanilla, and oloroso as well.

But Carla looked awful. Her face was lined and her body seemed to have sagged. She saw Alex's appraising look as she handed her her drink in a crystal glass.

'I hope it's how you like it.'

'Yes. Cheers.'

'Cheers.'

Carla met her gaze. 'I have expensive tastes.'

'Yes, you do. It's a lovely house. You look tired, Carla.'

'I'm exhausted.'

Alex felt nervous of saying any more, of appearing nosey. She stared into her glass.

'The last time we talked . . .'

'Yes, well I did it. I work three mornings a week. I am such a success with the clients they want me to work full time.'

'Good lord. But it's . . . all right? You don't mind it? You did think . . .'

'I hate it, Alex. I loathe it and detest it. I hate myself for it and it doesn't get better. I don't really need the money as much as that. All right I need more than I was getting, but for what I'm doing . . .'

'Then why don't you stop?'

'It's not as simple as that, is it? You know I have Selfridges food store deliver my goods – smoked salmon, what I like, the best drink. Franco can go to boarding school next year and I can be free. I can have a bigger car, take holidays. My life can be completely transformed. But I can't get used to it. They say I will, that I should stick it out. They're all like me, like us Alex. Women just like us; mothers, wives some of them, sweethearts; they're not perverts or oversexed or undersexed, just normal people.'

'Maybe you'll get used to it soon.'

'But do I want to get used to it, Alex? What's happening to me? Where does it stop that I can feel or suck the penis of a completely strange man every hour, put my finger up his rectum, make him come by . . .'

'Yes, well . . .'

Alex squirmed uncomfortably. It was just as she thought, after all. Penis, rectum, erection, vagina; the expressions would be correct and anatomical for Carla, no euphemisms, no willies or bum bums. She began to admire Carla and what she was doing, or rather why she was doing it.

'I really came because Milt asked me to. He is worried about you.'

'Oh I know. We met at the wrong time. He's a lovely boy. I like him . . .'

'He wants to marry you.'

'Isn't it *absurd*? I wouldn't dream of it. But I like him a lot. Another time . . .'

'Carla, why don't you stop now, as you said, and give it up? I'm not preaching, Carla, and in a way I admire you. But you do look awful, tired and unhappy and old. Before I would have said you couldn't possibly be 38, now you look well over 40. It must be corrupting, doing all those things, and money is corrupting too. Besides I want you to help me. It will sound absurd and, compared to your problems . . .'

'I? Can help you?'

'I want the basement flat. Itzhak Bar-Tur, you know my professor, wants to stay in England. He is very keen on the flat and I, well I'm keen to have him there too.'

'Oh good! Something went right after all!'

'Well nothing very much. Getting Itzhak interested is like landing a killer whale with some string and a safety pin. But I think he is keen, and having him near me will enable me to work on him.'

'You mean you've finally got over Harry?'

'Well . . . just about. He's getting married in a few weeks and having Itzhak about will help.'

'Yes I can see, but how . . . what can I do about the basement flat?'

'You could have Milt move in with you. He's crazy about you. It's what he wants, but he doesn't know how to say it.'

'You think I . . . But . . .'

Carla looked both angry and amazed and poured herself another drink.

'It would help you, Carla, wouldn't it? I don't think you'd ever break from the massage parlour otherwise. Why should you? You'd just go on getting more money and more blasé and bored, and older. What do you want, Carla? Is it what you want? What's the point? Franco would go to a smart boarding school and you'd hardly ever see him. He'd be a stranger to you, and then if he found out how his mother really lived, what would he say then? Oh yes they're women like us, but how do we know what they're really like, Carla? Inside?'

'You mean I should give it all up and have Milt . . .'

'But you like Milt, don't you? You may not love him but you like him a lot?'

Carla nodded.

'A lot. I'm crazy about the guy. But he's young, he's . . .'

'I'm not saying it's going to last or go on forever; but I think it's good for you at this moment.'

'But I needn't give up the massage parlour. He could come here anyway. I work mornings and he's at work.'

'But he'd know, Carla, wouldn't he? He'd want to know where the money came from. And full time? Why don't you give him a break, and you. Start again, Carla. I don't think the massage parlour suits you.'

Alex knew she was fighting as much for her own selfish interest as Carla's. She wanted Milt out of the flat and the only nice way she could get rid of him was like this. She wanted Itzhak by her, to help her get over the fact Harry was marrying another woman. It was happening at last.

Besides being tired, Carla couldn't analyse her emotions at this moment. But, yes, there did seem . . .

'Let me think it over,' she said. And then looking at the door at the sound of the bell. 'There's my patient. He's actually recovering from a broken back and I don't have to do anything but help him get better. I'll think about giving up the massage parlour.'

Carla gave Alex her old warm, friendly smile, that gay sexy look, and the years fell away from her. Suddenly Alex wanted Carla to have Milt living there for her own sake. She clasped Carla's strong arm and squeezed it, kissed her briefly on the cheek.

'Give it up, Carla. It's not worth it. It's not worth it for you, for your life. You don't really need to and it's changing you, spoiling you. Soon you won't even see the reason to stop and then it will all be too late.'

'Life gone?' Carla said, her head on one side. 'Maybe, I'll think about it. Thank you for being so straight, Alex.'

Alex walked back to her car feeling pleased. The old Alex would have got in a terrible muddle about this sort of situation and would have solved nothing; she would have been so busy seeing everyone's point of view.

The new Alexandra Twentyman was beginning to see things, oh, much more clearly.

13

Milt moved in with Carla, and Itzhak into the basement flat within a week of Alex's conversation with Carla. It was all done over the phone; Alex didn't know whether Carla had given up the massage parlour or not. Itzhak really precipitated things because he had to have somewhere to go quickly; the tenancy of his present furnished flat had expired.

At first, Alex behaved towards Itzhak as she would to any other tenant, except that the letting wasn't done through the agency but directly by her. It was very business-like with a letter of agreement, rent paid monthly in advance and so on.

Alex didn't want Itzhak to think she was getting him there solely to be with him. Just because she didn't want him to think this, she avoided seeing too much of him for the first few weeks.

But as well as bringing himself he'd brought her another manuscript, or rather introduced her to the source of one, if not many more. His publishers had admired the faultless typing of his *Demographic Survey of Europe 1880/1914*, and they thought they could give Alex as much work as she wanted.

So Alex was very busy seeing the publishers and meeting her next author, a lady historian whose subject was the City States of Ancient Greece.

Alex usually picked up Rachel from school, but Toby liked to go home on his own. One day, a week after Itzhak had moved in, Alex found Toby's form master Mr Jackson waiting for her in the playground, his face apologetic and solemn. Rachel came running anxiously towards her. Alex felt a paralysing sense of alarm. Toby had had an accident. Her hand clasped Rachel's convulsively.

'What is it, Mr Jackson?'

'The Head would like to see you in his room, Mrs Twentyman.'

'Is it about Toby?'

'I'm afraid it is.'

'Oh, what has happened, is he . . .'

'Toby's all right; he did have a fight but he only had a few scratches. He rather badly hurt someone else.'

'Toby hurt . . .?'

'Quentin Timperley.'

'Oh my God.'

'He's recovered, but he was unconscious for a few minutes and we had to call the doctor. He's been resting in the sick room.'

'*Toby* did this?'

'Mrs Richards will look after Rachel for you. She's waiting in the classroom.'

'How kind.'

The little procession wove its way across the playground and up the stone steps to the first floor classroom where Rachel was left with Mrs Richards. Then up the next flight to the Head's study, Alex aware of a sickening sensation of fear.

Inside the Head sat at his desk looking grave, Toby was standing by his side and a hysterical Fay Timperley was giving a personable imitation of one of the less well-balanced Furies.

'Now quiet, Mrs Timperley, please. Ah, Mrs Twentyman.'

At the magic name Fay turned round, her tear-stained face contorted with rage.

'I'm getting the police on to this. Never fear. You'll . . . you won't get away with *this*.'

The Head put a hand on Fay's arm which she snatched away glaring at him as though he had made some sort of attempt to molest her. Alex went and stood by Toby, briefly kissing him on the cheek.

'Are you all right, darling?'

Toby nodded miserably. He'd been crying too.

'Do sit down, Mrs Twentyman,' the Head indicated a seat. 'I'm sorry to have worried you like this.'

'*She's* worried . . .'

'*Please,* Mrs Timperley.'

'What happened exactly?' Alex said, longing for a cigarette.

'There was a fight in the playground. Apparently Quentin started it with some boys, but Toby is a big chap and he got the better of them.'

'Them? There were more than one.'

'Yes.'

'Then who's going to the police?' Alex said angrily looking at Fay.

'He's a big bully, a spoiled upper-class brat!' Fay snarled lighting the cigarette that Alex was longing for and spewing out smoke like tangible hatred.

'That's not fair, Mrs Timperley. Everyone says Toby was terribly provoked and lost his temper. It's true he is a big boy for his age. Normally I'd say shake and be friends, but Mrs Timperley indicates she wants to lodge charges with the police. I asked her to wait and see you.' The Head looked despairingly at Alex.

'Are you serious?'

Alex looked at Fay with amazement. But where would it end? Alex had no idea, having never had any contact with the police in her life.

'I am serious. I don't think louts should get away with it. He pummelled Quentin's head into the playground until he lost consciousness. He's mad.'

'That's not accurate,' Mr Jackson said with the air of one who has great patience and is frequently called on to exercise it. 'I was there. Quentin and some others were taunting Toby, who did nothing until Quentin threw a ball, quite a heavy one, in his face. This seemed to enrage Toby who jumped on Quentin and, yes, did bang his head into the ground rather heavily.'

'Had to have a *doctor* . . .'

'But why did no one intervene?'

'You know how these things are. Over quickly. I was at the far end of the playground when it started and when I got to them it was over . . .'

'My *Quentin* unconscious . . .'

'It was very unfortunate, and I hope Mrs Timperley won't go to the police. It was one of those things boys do . . .'

'. . . *every* intention of going to the police.'

Fay had never stopped muttering all during Mr Jackson's report, hardly bothering to listen to what he was saying.

'I'd better give my lawyer a ring,' Alex said firmly getting up and going to the phone. 'May I, Mr . . .'

At the word 'lawyer' Fay jerked her head up sharply. 'Who said anything about lawyers?'

'If my son is to be charged with some offence I must have my lawyer here immediately.'

If there was any class or profession Fay didn't like it was lawyers. She invested them with both distrust and a kind of awe, as though they dabbled in dark ritualistic practices she did not understand. She had had plenty to do with officialdom in her life, the police and the welfare; but any time lawyers had been involved, such as for her divorce, she'd been worsted. The thought of a lawyer . . .

'I haven't *quite* made up my mind about the police. I thought . . .'

There was almost a palpable feeling of relaxation of tension in the room. The Head even smiled. Mrs Timperley was one of the most troublesome mothers in the school and was in his office at least once a week complaining about some real or alleged mistreatment of her children either by staff or other children. He knew her background well and was sorry for her.

All heads looked up at a knock on the door which opened a crack and Lorna Galbraith popped her head in, smiling brightly.

'Mrs Richards had to go. I said I'd look after Rachel. Can she come home for tea? Oh Fay, you're here too.'

Whether Lorna knew or whether she was pretending not to know, Alex couldn't fathom; but she'd saved the situation. She seemed to realize the soothing effect of her presence and came into the room leaving Rachel outside the door.

'Is something awfully wrong? Can I help?'

At the sight of her benefactor Fay started crying and the Head gave one of his anguished glances to heaven and rapidly outlined what had happened.

'But is that *all*? And you're going to the *police*, Fay? How ridiculous. Do you remember the time Quentin brought his penknife out and ripped the jacket off . . .'

'Please!' said Fay abruptly ceasing to cry. 'Quentin has been hurt.'

'But it was an accident. He can be very provoking, you know. I think you must stop all this nonsense at once and come to tea with me. All of you. Even the Headmaster if he likes.'

The Head gazed gratefully at the secretary of the parents' committee, not for the first time thankful for her stalwart good sense, the authority she had over people.

'I won't if you don't mind, Lorna . . .'

'Then I'll take Fay and Alex and make them friends. Come!'

She gestured with such authority that Alex, who would much rather have gone home and talked to Toby, felt she couldn't refuse. She grimaced and got up.

'Well, but I would just like a word with the Head and Mr Jackson.'

'*What* is she going to say . . .' Fay began, but Lorna took her arm and propelled her to the door.

'Never mind; she just wants to talk. You accused her, you know, not the other way round. We'll get Quentin, and Alex can follow in her car. Come on Toby. Smile, lad!'

* * *

'Do you mind if I smoke?'

'Of course not, Mrs Twentyman.'

The Head bent forward to light her cigarette and Mr Jackson sat in the chair next to her.

'I am worried about Toby, you know. Worried that he should do this, however provoked. The old Toby would have walked away.'

'The old Toby?' The Head lifted his head interrogatively. 'The pre-Princess Maud Toby? Do you think he's deteriorated here?'

'He's different. I don't know if it's deterioration.'

'He's growing up, Mrs Twentyman, standing on his feet.'

'But it doesn't mean he should be banging the heads of his enemies into the ground until they lose consciousness. Supposing he'd have brain damaged, or . . . killed him.'

Alex gulped and took a strong drag at her cigarette.

'Are you worried about Toby generally? Mr Jackson?'

'No. He's very good at his work, ahead of the class. I feel he is frustrated though; he's got a super-abundance of energy. He should have far more things to do in his spare time. Does he do much at home, Mrs Twentyman?'

Alex thought of herself typing and Toby banging away in the upstairs room. She did nothing to organize his free time. She was aware now that she'd been shutting Toby out of her life, compartmentalizing him and Rachel.

'Well you know his father left home . . . I think that at The Heath Toby had more out-of-school activities.'

'Is he a cub?'

'No.'

'It's a bit late, but maybe he could have a year and then join the scouts. There are a lot of things Toby can do out of school if you want us to help you, Mrs Twentyman, but . . .' the Head paused and played with the paper knife on his desk, considering his words. 'I hope you don't mind me saying this, but I always get the impression you consider this school second best. You know what I mean? You were forced to leave the other schools and had to bring your children here.'

'I suppose that's true, if I'm honest.' Alex nodded and met his eyes. 'My friends do get at me a bit about it.'

'I thought they might,' Tom Bridge stood up and went to the window. 'You know, Mrs Twentyman, I don't consider this school second best to any and it isn't just because I am a devotee, a strong believer in a good state education for all. But I think we have a good school here; a balanced school. The staff are keen and the children bright and enthusiastic, not all but most.'

'What about Quentin Timperley?'

'Well he is one of the more difficult ones. But private schools have their difficult pupils too.'

'Quentin makes life hell for Toby, always has.'

'He's envious, don't you see? He admires him, wants to be like him. Could you try and make a friend of his mother, do you think?'

'*Me* a *friend* of hers? After this?'

'She's a very nice woman basically. A bit hysterical but very insecure. I know you're friendly with Lorna and she is too.

I think if we made her and her children feel more wanted, more part of the community, things would improve no end. Isn't that so, Brian?'

Mr Jackson nodded vigorously.

'Go back and have tea now, see what you can do. Think of it as a kind of duty as a member of the parents' committee. It might help you too. How can you be happy when you think your children aren't getting the best? I agree education is going through a terribly bad time in this country for which we have governments to thank, not teachers or children. We're the victims of their idiotic idealistic battles. But we need people like you and children like yours, and not the less able of society while the bright ones get creamed off into the private schools. It's a wicked system.'

Alex was impressed. It *was* a wicked system when you came to think about it. She decided to be very pro state schools and against private ones, like Lorna.

'But the place . . .' she said looking around.

'It's very old, but it is clean, bright and *happy*. The children never notice it, you know. Have your children ever complained about it?'

'No,' Alex had to agree. 'It's just me.'

'You're thinking of the rolling lawns of The Heath. I tell you Toby is a fine boy, he will do well wherever he is – but we must canalize that energy, harness all that pent-up creativity.'

Alex got up and smiled at the Head and Brian Jackson.

'I'm glad we had this talk. Maybe banging Quentin's head was a good thing.'

* * *

What Lorna minded most about Fay was that, although she was poor, she didn't *behave* poor; she didn't look poor; she smoked expensive cigarettes, she dressed well, was nicely made-up. What was more she was forever declining, politely but firmly, Lorna's gift of second, or even third-hand garments for herself or the children.

For Lorna jumble sales were among the greatest joys in her life. The very words JUMBLE SALE sent a thrill of excitement racing through her. She thought it must be something to do with buried treasure or the utter upper-middle class formality of her childhood where clothes automatically came from Debenham's or Harrod's and were uniformly clean and fitted well.

And although she'd always been wealthy, never known want, Lorna was mean; she liked to pay as little for something as she could. She clothed herself and most of the household, except George, from jumble sales. Even the dog's basket came from a jumble sale and most of the crockery in the kitchen. Such stringent economy, such a delight in jumble sales not only made Lorna feel better as a person – they made her feel she was being a good socialist too.

And here was Fay, moping about in some sort of fur coat with a neat woollen dress underneath which certainly had never come from a stall. Yes, and she got one of those long cigarettes out of that gold packet. God knew how much they cost. The trouble with Fay, in Lorna's opinion, was that she had no sense of priorities – good clothes and cigarettes came before finding somewhere decent to live. Moreover, instead of being grateful to a socialist government for providing all these necessary things of life, Fay was always telling the welfare authorities to get lost, or stuffed, or words of that description. There was no gratitude there, Lorna thought, either to the Labour Party, or people like herself who gave so much time and thought to the problems of people like Fay.

Toby and Quentin had been quite happy to make up as soon as they saw each other and were now upstairs with Sally, Amanda and Douglas. Fay was the problem, Fay and Alex.

They were in the kitchen, Lorna busy scraping margarine on bread for tea, Fay standing by the kettle waiting for it to boil when the front door opened. Lorna looked at the kitchen clock and then frowned.

'Funny. I didn't know we'd left it open. I wouldn't have expected Alex to be here so . . . George!'

George Galbraith, tall, good looking, well-dressed, the British Airways label fluttering from his hide executive case, stood in the doorway, the expression of good humoured bewilderment he always felt when he came home, on his face.

He could never get over the fact that he was married to this large untidy lady and that they had three large untidy children just like her, all clothed from the proceeds of jumble sales.

Also that he lived in this large untidy home and slept next to Lorna in a large untidy bed that got made about once a week.

Everything about George Galbraith was neat and meticulous. His suits, jackets and flannels were tailor-made; his shirts came from Turnbull and Asser in Jermyn Street and his hats from Lock's. He drove an XJ6 Jaguar that was always shiny and his huge office was the exact antithesis of his home – not a thing out of place.

Lorna and George had met at Oxford, undergraduates in their early twenties, keen idealists, fanatical socialists, both with wealthy backgrounds. Music, the arts, politics, reform, the rebuilding of Europe in the heady post-war years, everything had contributed to impel them towards each other. George was always handsome, conventionally so like a film star. Lorna was a strapping, wholesome sort of girl who eschewed make-up and was uninterested in clothes.

It seemed quite natural to marry as soon as they'd taken their finals; to live in one room in an old house on the Banbury Road which was always full of an argumentative mixture of young people. The student life continued while they took higher degrees and then split for George to go into industry and Lorna to get a job at the university. She moved to London ultimately to be with George. That was nearly twenty years ago.

They had both changed but they'd stayed together, not only through habit but affection, shared common interests. They were still socialists; they loved music, keenly followed the arts; most of their friends were celebrated in some field or other.

But George had grown even more handsome and distinguished looking, while Lorna had let herself go. The ideal was more important than the ego. She was quite unaware of how she looked, neither did she care; but her overweight, flaccid body repelled George and he found it difficult to make it with her in bed. He scarcely ever wanted to and neither did she. They were very fond companions.

Besides, George could put up with the unsatisfactory nature of his home life – Algerian plonk and endless spaghetti meals, the dirty house and the absence of sex – for two reasons: he was genuinely devoted to his wife and children and, more importantly, he was hardly ever there. He had made his life into what he wanted it to be, the international business scene, enabling him to get away from home as often as he could and, as a result, he was able to enjoy the good things about it when he returned.

'George!' Lorna flew up to him, breasts waving wildly, and planted a huge sisterly kiss on his cheeks. Lorna was still in love with her husband, but shy of him too. She had never quite got over her good fortune in someone as plain and ungainly as she attracting someone as elegant and suave as George. Because George was suave. He was tall and thin with sleek black hair, and he always had an attractive trace of eight o'clock shadow; he carried himself well. The fact that their sex-life was rare bothered Lorna very little. She approved of sex for other people, like Fay; thought it necessary for their physical and psychological well-being. But for Lorna it was no longer important in her life. She was always so busy now with a variety of intellectual things. Luckily it seemed the same with George. But although they discussed everything under the sun to do with politics, philosophy, psychology, music, modern art – the subjects were inexhaustible – they always avoided mentioning anything too personal, like sex.

'George, I didn't expect you back for a week.'

'I got bored with the conference. I was going on to Rio but decided to fly back. I've got to be off again next week anyway, and thought it would be nice to be home.'

Lorna's kind face creased with happiness.

'George, it's lovely to see you. You know Fay, don't you?'

Fay had immediately stopped lounging against the table when George came in and wished she'd seen to her face. Although her feelings about the male sex were so ambivalent, George Galbraith appealed to her. She thought she might change her mind if she had a man like him. She'd just been cursed with insipid unsexy people like Jack, or the sex fiend at work on account of whom she was going to have to leave. He'd started pawing her and never leaving her alone; he'd even tried to put a hand up her dress that very day. And now he was threatening that he'd find a reason to get rid of her despite the sex discrimination act, if she wasn't nicer.

The very thought of his fat, horrible, hairy, sweaty body on hers . . . Fay shuddered and George came up to her, a deep smile on his face.

'Of course. Fay how are you?'

Oh that smile. She could almost fall into his arms. If only she'd got someone like George . . .

'Well, we've had a bad day,' Lorna filled in for her. 'Quentin had a fight with Toby Twentyman at school and . . .'

'Toby Twentyman nearly *killed* Quentin,' Fay exploded.

'. . . anyway they're all right now. Can't you hear them upstairs, George?'

'A storm in a teacup.' George said smoothly. 'Do I know Toby Twentyman?'

'I don't think so, dear. They're new this year. Very sad. Father left home and the kids had to be removed from school etc. etc.'

'Alex Twentyman hasn't got a husband?' Fay said with interest. 'You mean she's on her own?'

'Yes just like you.' Lorna was brusque. 'You've never liked her, have you? That's because you don't let yourself know her. She's a nice girl. Ah there she is I think.'

'I'll go,' George said and went to the door.

Alex stared with amazement at this polished, handsome creature, the slightest whiff of expensive after-shave emanating from him as he opened the door. She imagined he must be one of the fathers picking up a child.

'Hello, you must be Mrs Twentyman. I'm just hearing all about the battle. Come in. I'm George Galbraith.'

The charmer extended a long cool hand which Alex shook with some bewilderment. George Galbraith. She had never for a moment imagined . . . why.

'Darling,' George called into the kitchen. 'I'll take Mrs Twentyman into the sitting room. Will you bring some tea?'

'Yes,' trilled a gay, girlish, excited voice.

'There,' George let down the blinds and switched on the low lamps that stood on tables about the room. 'Yes, I just came home today. I hear Sally is a friend of your daughter, but we seem to have missed meeting. I'm hardly ever here, I'm afraid.'

He gave her a pleasant smile and offered her a cigarette as the door opened and Lorna puffed in with a tray on which stood several assorted mugs, a large aluminium teapot purchased in a jumble sale, and a cracked plate of bread thickly spread with margarine. It looked like the sort of repast you would offer to a troop of unruly children. Alex noted George's excellent charcoal grey suit, white, white shirt and the edge of cuff that showed at his sleeves. Lorna had on a pair of very wide green slacks, badly stained down one leg as though one of the hamsters, or perhaps several, had had a nasty accident on it. The fly zip was broken and done up with two large safety pins and as she leaned over with the tray her dark nipples, clearly visible through the cheesecloth top, flicked across the top of the aluminium teapot making Alex fear again for a nasty accident, this time to do with burning. However, Lorna swooped aside in time and Alex breathed a sigh of relief. How did you deal with a scorched nipple and was it dangerous? She watched the pantomime as Lorna, talking nonstop, sloshed tea into the mugs, spilt the milk and upset the sugar on to the bread and marge, laughing uproariously as she offered it around.

'Sweet bread! There now, are we all happy? George darling, because I didn't know you would be here I have arranged to chair a meeting of the Gingerbread Group this evening. I . . .' she shrugged apologetically.

'That's quite all right, my love. I have a lot of things to do and it will be nice to see the children.'

'Well, Rufus is at a meeting of the Socialist Workers' Party, Doug has scouts and, yes, you can baby-sit with Sally.'

'That will be nice.'

'Now for tea I've left you . . .'

'Oh I think we'll pop round to the bistro,' George said quickly. One of his worst problems was having to accustom his delicate digestion to stodgy food after weeks of gourmet eating.

'Now, Alex and Fay, I want you to be friends,' Lorna said firmly. 'I know I'm putting my foot right in it; but you two women will like each other when you get to know each other. You have a lot in common.'

Alex wondered if this were not rather insulting to her, to be told she had so much in common with a woman she regarded as hostile and hysterical. However, she remembered her promise to the Headmaster.

'Perhaps I can drive you home?' she said, hardly believing

the words came from her own mouth, they were so much the opposite of what she had intended.

Fay's expression still hostile, was slightly mollified. 'That's kind of you, if it's not out of your way.'

* * *

Alex was appalled by the high-rise building and the broken down amenities, the walls stained with graffiti and the corridors smelling of urine. Although she hated heights she went up to Fay's flat and felt giddy as she looked down. The flat was comfortable enough, but there was so little room and already the children had started to fight as soon as they got in – Toby and Quentin breaking a temporary truce.

'My God, the din.' Fay placed her hands to her ears. 'I can hardly stand it at times. Here, I've got a bit of gin at the bottom of a bottle somewhere.'

Alex wanted to refuse but didn't like to somehow. Seeing Fay in this environment put her in a completely different context, so that what she herself had felt and experienced over the past two years seemed like mere self-indulgence.

'I hear your husband went off too,' Fay said passing her the glass.

Alex still resented the remark, the reduction of her own problem to some kind of common denominator, but she nodded.

'Well yes, he did.'

'Think he'll come back?'

'Oh no. He's getting married again.'

Fay looked at Alex and her plump nervous face underwent a sudden and unexpected transformation – grief and spite and the cold irrational dislike she felt for Alex were muted into a feeling of sisterly togetherness.

'Oh, I feel sorry for you. Although I hated Jack I couldn't believe it when he actually went and got married. It was an awful time. To think of him leaving me like that, and the children, and then actually being *happy* again. I couldn't stand it. It's the worst thing of all, but it does get better.'

Alex too was surprised at the unexpected change, the abandonment of hostility. Fay drew her chair up to sit close to Alex.

'If I can do anything let me know. I have a lot of my own troubles, largely brought about by myself, I know . . .'

'Oh . . .' Alex began.

'No don't say it. I know it's mostly me. I'm so tense, you see. Because I'm shy people think I'm hostile and it makes me worse. I know you thought I was unfriendly. I'm just shy.'

'I understand,' Alex said. 'I'm a bit shy too; people think I'm snobby and I'm not.'

'There, isn't that extraordinary!' Fay impulsively patted Alex on the lap. 'We've both got this problem. People don't understand, do they? I was always nervous and I married to get some protection. It was silly, because I didn't. I was only 18 when I married Jack, and made the mistake I've been paying for ever since. We didn't get on in bed, you see. Never. He used to throw himself on me, he had no technique. We were both virgins and it was awful. I used to say, "why don't you get a book and learn about it for God's sake?" But he said it was my fault, that I was unresponsive. God knows why I married him.'

'Why did you?' Alex said contrasting this with her own happy experience.

'I wanted to get away from home. I was a clerk-typist at the local employment office. I lived in a fantasy world because everything around me was so drab. My mother had been left and it wasn't easy. We lived in a tiny terraced house and all started work at 15. It was a grimy, ugly northern town and I wanted to be anywhere but there. Jack worked in the same office as I did and he fancied me at once. He said he could get a transfer to London if I married him. I wasn't very struck with him, he wasn't at all good looking – you've seen him now and he was worse then – age has improved him. But that did it. London! I thought everything would be all right just to be away from home, in London! All the girls envied me getting married and going away; but it was all a silly dream. It never went right.'

'And then he left?'

'Well, not suddenly. He kept on saying he would. After

Amanda was born I said I didn't want any more children and I wouldn't have sex with him again at any price. I just refused to. He got so wild he beat me about a bit and it was hell I can tell you. Then he started not coming home, having affairs. I didn't care as long as he left me alone, but we had awful rows as well and it made the kids unhappy. Then he met this girl, the one he's married to, and just left. He sent a letter to say he wasn't coming home any more; then he said he had a nervous breakdown – although I never believed him – and went into hospital. We had no money and we had to leave where we were living. I had an awful time until Lorna Galbraith helped me. Lorna has a lot of faults, but she does have a heart of gold.'

'Yes, she has,' Alex said. 'Most separations come after a gradual wearing down. When they happen you really expect them. I think that's the difference between my situation and so many others. I didn't.'

'You didn't expect it at all?'

'No. I thought we were very happy. But he was having an affair and I didn't know. Didn't even have a glimmer of suspicion.'

'Oh that *is* terrible, not to know. I knew quite well with Jack; he told me. "Go ahead and screw them," I said to him, "but for God's sake leave me alone." He did. How do you feel about your husband now?'

'Better,' Alex said slowly.

'Is there anyone else?'

'Not . . . quite.' Alex smiled.

'Not quite. That's a funny expression. You mean you like him, but he's not hooked?'

'Yes, I think he likes me, but he's shy. Carla says I have to lead him on a bit more.'

'Ah, Carla. She is the one who knows all about sex. She's always trying to persuade me to, well, let myself go. I don't seem to have the way with men that Carla has.'

'I don't either!' Alex laughed.

'I think I'm frigid – I've hardly ever had an orgasm – but Carla says I haven't been woken by the right man. She says no woman is inherently frigid. I just don't like it. Do you?'

Alex could never remember having such frank discussions about sex with women she hardly knew, as she had since the children had been at Princess Maud's. It seemed the key topic of conversation at all levels.

'Yes, I do. I miss it.'

'You haven't, since your husband?'

'Just once, on holiday. But nothing since . . .'

'That must be hard if you want it but can't get it. I like men, you know, but not sex. I think it's disgusting, horrible,' Fay made a grimace of distaste, then looked at Alex as if wondering if she could trust her to keep a secret. 'You know who I do fancy? Who does turn me on every time I see him?'

'Who?'

'George Galbraith. Now if any man might make me like sex it would be him. Don't you think he's fantastic?'

'He's attractive,' Alex concurred. 'The last person I would have thought . . .'

'For Lorna. They've been married for years, adore each other. I can't understand it, though I love Lorna. I wonder she doesn't try more to make herself attractive for him.'

'Well, if it's not important to him . . .'

'But it must be, don't you think? You should see Lorna at the old clothes stall at the summer fair. She's the first there and buys the family's clothes for a year, yet George goes to Savile Row.'

'People are curious.' Alex stood up. 'Thanks Fay. I'm glad we got together after all. I'm sorry about Toby.'

'Oh, forget it. Of course I know he was provoked. I'm just so tense all the time, worried about my job, living here, the kids are so naughty, out of hand. I could go mad at times. I really could. All alone up here on top of the world. Still I'm glad we had the chance to talk. You never really know a person do you? I thought you were so stuck up and superior and you're just shy – like me.'

'That's right. I'm not superior at all, not in any way. I'd love us to be friends, Fay. Look get your diary and we'll make a date for Quentin to come to tea next week, and maybe you can come to dinner.'

'What do I do about the other kids? Ralph's all right, but Amanda is only 7. She's out for tea today.'

'Bring her . . . Bring her and Quentin, she'll be company for Rachel.'

Alex was getting a headache from the din the children were making. She noticed Fay had been quietly tipping up the bottle of gin into her glass as they talked. She couldn't blame her. It was a hell of a life yet she was bright, attractive, bitter. Alex supposed that what she needed was a man to bring her back to life. Which brought Alex back to her siege of the reluctant Itzhak.

14

Alex knew when she woke up that the day was bad. A bad day. The depression lay on her head, on her chest and her limbs making them heavy and painful, difficult to move. She just wanted to lie and, immobile, gaze at the ceiling, the white restful ceiling, forever.

Alex turned her head and looked at the smooth uncrumpled half of the bed. Harry's half. He would never come back to it now.

It was Harry's wedding day. She had been dreading it more than any visit to a hospital, a doctor, a dentist or an irascible employer – any visit where one dreaded the diagnosis and the outcome. Yet as with such visits she had pretended it was not going to happen; as she'd gone about the normal tasks of daily life – school, cleaning, typing, cooking – for the last few weeks she had tried to put this day out of her mind, as far away as possible.

Now that it was here she had pills in plenty, but still no support or comfort, nothing to replace Harry.

Of course technically she hadn't been married to Harry for some weeks, since the divorce became final. In reality she hadn't been married to him for eighteen months – he'd been no husband, no companion, not much of a friend. He'd excised her from his life with the swift irrevocability of a surgeon's knife – to use the hospital metaphor again. There had been no grey in-between stage with Harry.

At that moment, the antithesis to despair, an object of supreme happiness, Rachel, danced into the room.

'Oh Mummy, I'm so excited. I can't *wait* for the wedding, can you?'

She hurled herself on to her mother's bed, a small bundle

of dark hair, olive skin and white flowing nightie. A beauty. Alex stroked her head as she huddled against her mother's chest.

Although Harry continued to see the children, there was something perfunctory in the way he did it. He seemed to think that seeing them was all that was required of him – his physical presence was enough. Apart from that he never enquired about their welfare, their activities or their school. Alex wished he would come to the school with her from time to time to see the class teachers once a term when they made their reports on the children's work. But Harry had never been to the school; he didn't even know where it was. Just because he didn't live with them he no longer seemed to consider himself in any way responsible for them.

'Oh Mummy I can't *wait* for it to happen; aren't you excited?'

'If you're talking about your father's wedding to Rosalind, not very.'

Rachel looked anxiously up at her mother, nuzzled closer. 'Are you sad about it?'

Alex didn't know how to reply, honestly, not now. She was not excited and she was not sad – what was the word to describe how she felt?

Angry.

That was it: she was angry that the thing had to happen, at the mess Harry had made of her life. But also angry that he wasn't coming back, that he was gone forever. She couldn't tell Rachel she was angry. This was a sort of game that sophisticated people played and it would not do to get back to Harry. She kissed Rachel and began getting out of bed.

'I'm not sad. I'm not happy. It's just something that must be gone through. Hurry or you'll be late.'

For some perverse reason Rosalind wanted a service of blessing after her registry office wedding; no doubt, Alex reasoned, to appear virtuous in the sight of the Lord after she had coolly and carefully deprived Alex of a husband. Thus the children were going through both ceremonies, and to lunch at the Hyde Park Hotel, and then the Draxes were taking them home for the rest of the day out of some unexpected consideration for Alex's feelings.

Alex went through the motions of feeding Toby and Rachel, getting them into their best clothes and waiting for the Draxes to arrive on the doorstep at ten o'clock which they did, on the dot.

Roger stayed in the car but Emma, a dazzle of furs, jewels and expensive scent, flashed out on to the pavement and into the house.

'I must spend a penny, darling,' she said loudly, beckoning to Alex frantically. Emma went into the lavatory in the hall and left the door open so she could talk to Alex.

'I've got the most fantastic job, writing copy for an advertising agency. You remember that plain little Harriet Fleischman?'

Alex could hardly recall the convent school, it all seemed such a long time ago.

'Oh yes, came to school in a Rolls . . .'

'*That's* it. Well, after Rachel left, Harriet became Portia's best friend and Charlie Fleischman . . . well I think he rather likes me. In fact I know he does. A lot.'

Alex wished she could see Emma's face. The excited girlish whisper gave so little of the truth away, whereas her face was normally quite easy to read.

Scrape of paper, flush, sound of running water, hands being washed. Pulling her skirt down Emma appeared at the door of the lavatory her face alive with excitement and mischief. She looked very pretty, Alex thought, plain no longer. Perhaps Roger had made her plain all those years.

'Yes, Charlie Fleischman. He's a *millionaire*! £15,000 a year to write copy for one of his agencies.'

'£15,000!' Alex was both jealous and appalled. 'But you've had no experience!'

'Of course I haven't.' Emma winked. 'It's for services rendered. I'm dying to tell you all about it. Now I must dash. We'll bring the kids back about nine. Try not to feel it too much, darling. He's an awful swine and quite unworthy of you.'

'I can't understand why you're going to the wedding.'

'Oh, *noblesse oblige*, all that public school rot. Not content with Harry pushing him in the mire, Roger now wants Harry to see him rolling in it. He thinks he'll be accused of sulking and losing face if he doesn't go.'

'Has Roger got a job yet?'

Emma's excited expression at the prospect of her own good fortune was replaced by one of boredom at the thought of Roger's hardship.

'My dear don't ask, or rather ask if you must, but forgive me if I'm not exactly enthusiastic. He's going to manage one of those dreary little wine chain stores. A *tiny* little place in Finchley. What a come down; of course Roger has got no initiative. Darling we'll get together very soon and I'll tell you all about Charlie Fleischman. The main thing,' she called heading for the door, 'is that Portia won't have to leave the convent.'

Alex got to the door just as Emma tumbled into the car still talking. The three children were waving enthusiastically from the back window.

The only one who didn't look happy was Roger. He didn't wave at all, or even smile.

* * *

Alex was wrong in thinking that Itzhak Bar-Tur was indifferent to her; he was very susceptible indeed, had been from the beginning, but he had been uncertain of her feelings. Her calm, cool, statuesque English beauty seemed to confirm what Lorna had told him: she was still desperately in love with her own husband. Itzhak, a philosopher rather than a fighter, thought what could you do with that kind of opposition? So he gave up before the struggle began and pretended a kind of indifference to Mrs Twentyman that he was far from feeling.

But the notion to move into the downstairs flat had been his when she'd told him one evening that her divorce had come through. She still seemed as immune to him as ever, but he thought if he could get a little closer she might unbend.

He had thought of her a great deal during the months he'd been seeing her, looked forward so much to those business-like visits just to look at her, or feel her warm, soft body near him. It was a very womanly body, delicately perfumed and enticing in its smells. Very different from Hannah's thin, angular almost masculine body.

But Mrs Twentyman never gave him any hope at all until

the day she let him call her Alexandra and after that he'd determined to try and get the basement flat. And it had been so easy; he'd concocted a lie about having to move out of his and she had almost kicked the poor American boy into the bed of his mistress. Itzhak had never seen such speed, but all parties had been more than willing – Alex to have him, Milt to be kicked into the mistresses bed, and Carla to receive him there. Itzhak and Milt had even become quite friendly in the process, despite its swiftness, although most conversation was limited to Milt extolling the virtues of his girlfriend, apparently a physiotherapist and a wizard between the sheets as well.

Itzhak wanted to bring the whole thing now full circle, as it were, to round it off so that he and Alex Twentyman could enjoy the delights of carnal knowledge too.

To that end he watched with great interest the arrival of the Draxes to spirit away the Twentyman children, knowing quite well they were attending their father's wedding. Then at noon, after carefully completing his toilet and carrying a bottle of Kosher wine, he went up and rang Alex's bell.

* * *

After the children left, Alex wanted to go back to bed; she had dressed to receive the Draxes, not wishing to appear a slut – she had been all neat in jeans and a shirt, fully made-up, trying to look as though she didn't really care.

But she cared. She wanted just to go back to bed and stay there. It occurred to her to call a friend, but who? Lorna, Carla and Fay worked and the other mothers she knew even less well than them; apart from the Draxes she kept in touch with none of the mothers from the convent. If no one else made the effort, you didn't feel like it either. Not even with Natasha Pont who had been so nice.

No, she wouldn't go back to bed. She'd do something about the garden, maybe. It was a lovely spring day for Harry's wedding (Rosalind having arranged it of course). No. no the garden would be too full of symbols of life and fertility and depressing things of that nature, that Alex didn't care to be reminded of on this particular day.

She tidied the kitchen, made the beds, hoovered and then

got herself some coffee and took it into the sitting room. She stretched herself on the couch so that she could see the sky but not the garden; the dust spots flickered in front of her eyes. She shut them and then opened them again quickly because all she could think about was her and Harry's wedding day.

She had a clear cinematographic image of it, every moment from the time she woke in the morning to the moment, full of champagne and rich food, they'd gone to bed in the hotel near the airport at night. Not that they hadn't been to bed before, which was just as well because, owing to the champagne, Harry's performance was not up to its promises. She'd had a messy and dissatisfying wedding night which had been forgotten in the very good time they'd had on the honeymoon, with Harry rested, not always so drunk and in full vigour.

Maybe that wedding night had been an omen; yes, after all these years it came vividly back to her now as a symbol of the ultimate failure of the marriage.

The ring at the door startled her from her reverie. The postman surely? Maybe a telegram of sympathy from Harry? Nearly noon. The marriage would almost be over; or maybe it was and, like some talisman, God's blessing was about to be sought from the vicar of the church in Putney.

Itzhak Bar-Tur stood on the doorstep, a bottle of Kosher wine in his hand, an expression of . . . well, shyness, sympathy on his face? Hard to tell.

It was an awkward moment. They stared at each other and then he half offered her the bottle and when she reached out a hand to take it, withdrew it.

'Oh I'm sorry . . .'

'Oh I'm sorry . . .'

Confusion, staring, laughter. She knew then why he had come.

'I know it's not very good wine,' Itzhak said wiping his feet neatly on the doormat. 'In fact it was a present from a friend of mine who is very orthodox. I don't know anything about wine and thought champagne would not be . . .'

He gave her a nervous glance and his dark skin went darker.

'Itzhak, you've come to cheer me up. You darling.'

Darling . . . Itzhak began to tremble inwardly at the word.

Of course it was a very common English expression 'darling', but to think of Alexandra using it . . . well, it was the last thing he'd expected so soon.

'Why not champagne?' Alex said boldly. 'Let's celebrate getting rid of Harry.'

He went into the sitting room and looked about him, remembering the first time he'd entered it. He'd liked the place at once. Now it looked strange and unfamiliar as though he'd never been there before. It had an aura about of . . . expectancy? He heard Alex in the kitchen and then she came in with the wine and two glasses on a tray, and a corkscrew and a plate of stuffed olives.

'I'm sorry about the wine . . .'

'Itzhak, I don't want to hear about the bloody wine again. I don't care what it's like, I'm not Harry. It was very sweet of you . . . very *kind*.'

Kind, that was the thing Harry was not. He wasn't thoughtful; he didn't remember birthdays or bring you tea when you were ill. He wasn't cruel, the opposite of kind, but he wasn't thoughtful. She simply hadn't expected from Harry that sort of thing, which was why she always had to keep control so much and remain self-sufficient.

'Are you . . . upset?'

'You know it's Harry's wedding day?'

Alex drew the cork with her customary expertise and absent-mindedly tasted the wine.

'I saw the children dressed in their finery, Rachel in a long dress, very pretty. She's a lovely girl. I'm very sorry, Alexandra. Sorry, about . . . well, I never knew him, but I know you're, um . . .'

Alex looked at Itzhak and the tears came into her eyes. Could anyone make up for the kind of loss she felt about Harry? Could any words *help*?

'He was a bastard!' she said fiercely. 'I can't understand why I ever loved him so much, or how. You can't explain those things can you? You know I've thought so much about Harry these months since he left and I've analysed him and hated him, but . . .'

'There's a kind of love left,' Itzhak said.

'Yes, that's it, a kind of love. You're quite right, Itzhak, something you try and destroy but can't.'

'It goes eventually,' Itzhak said, wishing she'd sit beside him on the sofa and the bulk of his weight would make her sink towards him. 'I never told you about my wife Hannah.'

'Itzhak I didn't even know you were married.'

Awful sinking feeling, blow to add to blow. Of course the reason he had never made advances to her was that he was married; but . . . why, it stood to reason that they were separated or something. He saw the concern on her face and misjudged the reason for it.

'Well, my wife Hannah couldn't stand leaving Israel. She hated the Jews of the Diaspora, well not hated them exactly, but didn't think they were true Jews.

'She became fanatical about it really. She was born a Sabra in Israel, like me, but I never felt the same way as Hannah. To me Jewry was universal. She didn't see that for my work it was necessary to travel abroad. At first she came to the States, then she went back, and then I went to see her to talk about things . . . but she would never leave Israel again. It was no sort of marriage.'

'It must have been awful.'

Alex assumed a tragic expression, hoping the relief in her voice would not show. What a very good thing it was that Hannah had been so reluctant to leave Israel.

'Well, there were other incompatibiilties, which I won't go into now and then Hannah wanted to marry again – a man working in the kibbutz where she was living. They're still there I think.'

'Married?'

'Oh yes, two or three children or something. But it did take me a long time to get over Hannah. She was very beautiful, very intelligent. I couldn't believe she didn't love me enough to want to share my life.'

'And you didn't love her enough to give it up.'

Itzhak paused in the act of raising his glass to his lips and looked at her.

'Pardon?'

'Well, you see, Itzhak, since Harry left and meeting all these women at the school on their own – women like me – I've had to think a lot. Harry just moved out of here and left me with total responsibility for the kids when, after all, they are as much his as mine; but with only half a life. I'd never had a career, never done anything that wasn't centred on my family. Harry had a girlfriend, a business he was very interested in. I had nothing to take my mind off what he'd done. It wasn't my fault. I'd chosen "housewife" as a profession. And all the other women I've met – in similar circumstances – have been more or less the same.'

'It's because a woman's life is centred on the home,' Itzhak said, 'I know what you're trying to say. The woman is still expected to make the sacrifices. Hannah resented that too. She was a chemist and wanted to be a doctor. Our roles were very difficult in our marriage. But more than anything . . . oh let's talk about something other than Harry or Hannah. Let's . . .'

Itzhak had a curious expression in his eyes, and he turned towards Alex who sat in a chair opposite him, his heavy body swinging awkwardly on the sofa. 'Come and sit beside me.'

Alex felt terribly nervous all of a sudden. Heavens was he . . .? But, held by the power of his eyes, she got up and went and sat beside him and, as he turned, the whole sofa sank as they'd both known it would and she fell almost on top of him. This time though she stayed there and the drink, fallen from her hand, made a dark patch on the pale carpet as all the kosher wine emptied out on to it.

* * *

Ever afterwards Alex remembered Harry's wedding day as the day she and Itzhak became lovers quite suddenly after she'd landed on top of him; no messing about with words or elaborate removal of clothes but basic and fundamental, a release of suppressed passion, and over very quickly, on the floor.

It was a nice satisfying experience to blot out Harry's treachery from her life; it seemed to make up for what Harry had done. She remembered that afterwards they'd lain on their backs side by side only half dressed, odd garments scattered over the floor. The lack of finesse had seemed to make it more intimate.

It was an odd way, she'd thought, to begin a love affair, lacking the sort of formal niceties that she'd imagined a person like Itzhak would go in for – low lights, lots of chat, awkwardness, Itzhak being so clumsy, and any amount of fore-play. But not at all. When it came to it, Itzhak had proved extraordinarily decisive, going expertly right to the point, as it were, sensing her own need was just as great as his and that she was ready for him.

Itzhak was very surprising. You really didn't know a man until you'd had sex with him, Alex decided, looking sideways at his satisfied, thoughtful face. She did hope he wasn't going to start apologizing and explaining their behaviour away, but he didn't.

'It was destined,' he said at last, 'from the day I stepped inside this house.'

'Then think what we've been missing all this time,' Alex said smiling at him.

'But I thought . . .'

'And I thought . . .'

He silenced her by turning and taking her in his arms, embracing her tenderly. Then his eyes closed and he fell gently asleep, his face very close to hers, his hand around her bare thigh. She looked with interest at his long thick penis and its purple circumcised tip; she'd never had sex with a circumcised man before. Harry's foreskin was intact. He said nature intended it that way and she'd believed him.

There was so much about her ex-husband, what he did, what he said, that Alex had taken as gospel for so many years and in this, she decided, snuggling against her new lover, as in so much else, Harry was proving very fallible indeed.

15

The summer term, unlike that record-breaking summer the year before, was cold and wet and everyone kept asking when the good weather was to come. Alex kept the children in winter clothes until May. But things like this apart, the weather was quite unimportant for Alex that year because her developing relationship with Itzhak completely occupied her attention.

That they'd wasted all those months in misunderstanding was something they gradually discovered, and that they'd both resorted to the same ploy – the basement flat – to get together was laughed about a lot. The basement flat became their love nest so that the children would not be suspicious and Alex still slept alone in her large bed every night, except sometimes when Itzhak would come to bed with her, but left after making love.

Itzhak was in extremely good form the whole of that summer and what delighted Alex so much was how versatile he was compared to Harry. Of course she hadn't had the experience of someone like Carla, and she realized how naïve it had been to judge the whole of the sexual performance of mankind by one single man. Now that she knew so much more she thought she and Harry had had rather a dull sex life really. Of course, Itzhak was cosmopolitan; he had travelled about.

What surprised Itzhak was how randy his pure English rose really was, a delightful pleasure after he had seriously considered the possibility of frigidity. Here they were both in their thirties, he nearly 40, cavorting about like young puppies at all times of the day and night, because it wasn't possible to have the regulation bedtime as most conventionally married couples had. They'd make love before Itzhak went to college, or when he came back if he had an early lecture and before the children came home. Or late at night after the children were in bed. It was like beginning life all over again.

The thing that worried Alex, or rather didn't worry her enough, was contraception. She'd stopped the Pill when Harry left home because she'd thought it was time she stopped it anyway for health reasons. Itzhak assumed, apparently, she *was* on the Pill but you had to wait a certain time before you could start taking it again and she hadn't liked to tell him this, to spoil their love-making.

When she told Carla she was horrified.

'But if you make a baby your romance will be killed!'

'I don't care really. You know I'd like another baby anyway.'

'But, Alex, this is foolish. You never talk with him about it?'

'Of course not. We're not teenagers. He assumes I take the precautions.'

'Then you must go straight to the doctor!'

But Alex didn't go to the doctor; she liked the idea of playing with fire. Maybe have Itzhak's baby? Her renewed sex life made her feel so fertile, so ready to breed.

She saw a lot of Carla during the summer because they helped arrange the Summer Fair. So did Fay Timperley and so did Lorna. The four now were thought of as firm friends. Between them, under the guidance of the capable Lorna, they organized the Summer Fair into an event of unusual splendour with Alex writing to people to ask for free gifts for the raffle and tombola and organizing publicity, Carla marshalling voluntary helpers, and Fay undertaking to look after the catering.

Although all the women blossomed that summer, especially Alex and Carla who had started new love-affairs, it was particularly noticeable that not only had Fay improved, but the whole of her brood as well. After having his head bashed by Toby Twentyman, Quentin became a disciple and was part of the Twentyman Gang, which exercised considerable power and control in the playground at recreation periods. He had also stopped needing special coaching. Ralph, who had always been exemplary anyway, obtained a scholarship to a private boarding school which horrified Lorna, but which everyone else thought was necessary and good for Ralph's personal advancement.

Fay didn't stop fighting people, or being aggressive in the butcher's or supermarket because, until the opposite was proved, she tended to regard all mankind as hostile. But once friendship was established, and Fay needed friends so badly for her security, she couldn't do enough for the recipients of her regard – such as Lorna and Carla and Alex.

The women took to helping one another out so that they could cope with their work, the Summer Fair and looking after the children. They devised a rota whereby the kids went to the houses of either Lorna, Carla or Alex after school – Fay being exempt because of the difficulties of the high-rise flats.

Anyway Fay was working full time at the gas board. She'd got a job there after a particularly unpleasant scene with her ex-employer which had involved a scuffle, a disordered office and the brandishing of a paper knife by Fay to prevent his coming any closer.

Carla had left the massage parlour just as she was beginning not to mind it. It appeared that it was true, after all, that you could get used to anything; especially a hard-headed Italian peasant girl like her. It was true that you did settle down; the work became routine, you developed your favourite clients rather as you had some patients for physiotherapy you preferred to others. Even the ones you didn't like you coped with, and then there was the camaraderie, the friendliness among the girls. There were things Carla felt she would miss about the massage parlour, but she left not only because Alex had said she looked older – and Carla was vain – but because her involvement with Milt had deepened and she was afraid of what he might do if he found out.

A not unimportant factor also was that he was a wealthy boy, apparently his father was a big name in oil in the States, and he was able to contribute substantially to the housekeeping so that she could maintain the style of life she liked – the Selfridges van and that sort of thing. Milt liked living well too. The only negative aspect of the affair was that Milt didn't get on too well with Franco, who bitterly resented his living there and going to bed with his mother. The idea of a boarding school now began to have substance.

Carla parted from the massage parlour leaving friendly relations with the management and a lot of satisfied clients behind her. Both hoped that she would soon come back. It wasn't every day you got a girl so good with her hands, so versatile in every way.

The day of the Summer Fair was fraught with anxiety on many counts. It had rained early in the day, the clouds were low and hovering exactly over the school playground, the celebrated TV personality who had been persuaded to give his services free decided he couldn't, and Lorna felt rotten with a summer cold.

However, by mid-afternoon the sun was blazing down, the food was almost sold out, a record capacity had attended to raise money for the school and the event was judged a success by any standards.

At the close Lorna had lost her voice, Itzhak who had manned the tombola was exhausted, so were Carla and Milt who had done the hoopla, and Alex who had been general dogsbody. Fay was quite fresh because she had done the least, and all the children were as agile as though they had just woken up in the morning.

Yet the place had to be cleared up and the hall made ready for the parents' dance that night. The beautiful show of children's work, the painting, the embroidery, the pottery had all to be put away and bunting and streamers positioned; the bar to be set up in a corner.

It had been decided that all the children would spend the night at Lorna's because Rufus would keep an eye on them and leave the parents free to go to the party. This was going to be fun too and made the children even more boisterous and noisy. But at the end of the day Lorna had had enough. She would stay at home nursing her cold and she insisted that George, who had been such a stalwart at the ice cream stall, should escort Fay to the dance in her place.

Fay couldn't get over her good fortune. George Galbraith to herself. Of course nothing would happen, how could it? She was so loyal to Lorna. He probably didn't fancy her anyway . . .

George Galbraith was more than exhausted at the end of the day of the Summer Fair. He'd been at home for nearly a month and everything was getting him down – the ceaseless noise, the meetings, the plans for meetings, the meetings that were actually held in the house, the slapstick dinners or no dinners at all, the filth, Lorna refusing to employ a cleaner because no real socialist would have another comrade working in a menial capacity, and the chaos.

Worse, George had been offered the deputy chairmanship of the company which would mean far less travel abroad, far less opportunity to get away from home. But to turn down the deputy chairmanship would mean abandoning his career, his future in this company and if he moved it was doubtful whether he could do as well, the company who valued his services so much had seen to that.

It was thus in a bad, truculent frame of mind that George changed and joined in all the noise and chit-chat that preceded the dance to be held at the school at 8.30 that evening. Everyone noticed how silent George was, how far from his usual sunny self. Was he ill? Was he worrying about business?

No, George was worrying about the fact that he hadn't tried, long ago, to face the reality of his home life; the unsatisfactory physical side of his marriage to Lorna, which suddenly seemed so important now that he couldn't get away. No amount of friendly affection made up for sleeping in the same bed, night after night, with a woman you couldn't make love to. He should have done something about it years ago instead of ignoring it.

Alex and Itzhak, Carla and Milt drove in one car to the dance, having changed at the Galbraiths' amidst more chaos and confusion than anyone could remember, more shrieking of children, noises, thumps and bangs than any of them liked to recall. They were all rather shattered when they got to the party and Itzhak, for one, wanted to abandon the idea and go home with Alex to spend the whole night in bed together – a chance they rarely had. But no one could think of foregoing the dance; they were on the parents' committee. They were also there *in loco* Lorna.

George drove Fay silently to the dance, so silently she thought he didn't want to take her, that he didn't like her, resented her. Then he couldn't find a parking space and that made things worse, and as soon as they got upstairs he made for the bar and she thought she wouldn't see him again – he just disappeared amid a crowd of heavy masculine shoulders, arms busily raising glasses to thirsty lips.

'See how pretty Fay looks tonight,' Alex told Carla as they waited for the men to bring back their drinks, calling Fay to join them too. 'She looks out of sorts though.'

Fay did look pretty. Her burnished hair was nearly shoulder-length and was combed straight back from her forehead, secured by a black ribbon. She had on a dark chiffon gown and very high heeled shoes to make her look taller; her make-up was perfect and her eyes sparkled after using special drops.

'I wish she had a man,' Carla said. 'I really do.'

And then George Galbraith emerged from the throng carrying two glasses, one of which he gave to Fay who had waved to her friends from the other side of the hall, but not joined them.

'Oh,' she said with surprise. 'For me?'

'Only red or white wine I'm afraid, or beer. You didn't want beer did you?'

'No. Thank you very much.'

'Whew what a day.' George gave a loud sigh and smiled. He looked about him, waved to one or two of the people he knew, looked to see if there were any attractive single women, no . . . turned to look at Fay. He took a second look at Fay. She was almost transformed, he thought. He'd never noticed her being as pretty as this. In fact, he'd always thought her too plain and a bit too fat. She invariably looked pale and careworn, hunched up somehow. Also her personal life was such a mess, the children continually being got out of trouble. Lorna having to do this, that and the other.

'How are the children?' he said.

'The children?' Fay taken by surprise at the remark. 'You saw them tonight.'

'Of course. Not in any trouble, are they?'

'Oh no George, they've vastly improved.'

'Good. That's fine. You look well too.'

Fay had noticed, couldn't help noticing, how George Galbraith had started to stare at her. She was glad she'd paid all that money for the slim fitting chiffon, hocked all next week's pay, had her hair coloured and restyled, had a facial. George Galbraith made her feel a woman – and just now a beautiful, attractive woman, with a slender alluring figure.

'Let's dance,' he said suddenly, putting his glass on a bench, taking hers and putting it next to his, and taking her in his arms.

* * *

George Galbraith lay with his head resting on his hands looking out of the window of the high-rise flat. At night it really was very spectacular, the view of London, the bright red glow of the West End in the sky. In the dark it was cosy and beautiful, not sordid at all.

'How long have you lived here?'

'About five years,' Fay said, 'since Jack did the flit. We had a nice furnished flat before then with a balcony, but he wouldn't keep up the rent.'

'What a swine.'

'He just left us and took off with this woman, then pretended he was ill so we were all on social security.'

'It must have been very hard for you, Fay.'

George turned towards her and kissed her tenderly. He had seldom felt such a rapport with a woman in such a short time. It was almost as though he'd fallen in love with her at the party, though of course he hadn't; he'd just become aware of her and he'd very urgently wanted her body – this taut, pleasant, petite womanly body that lay naked beside him now. Plump, true, but not wobbly and ungainly like Lorna's – that had really gone to seed. Her breasts were large, but firm and erect, not half-way down to her waist like Lorna's, and every bit of her was well made and nicely developed, in proportion.

Fay gave herself without restraint to George and his embrace, responding eagerly as she never had before, enjoying his weight, the feel of him between her legs. She drew them together to try and trap him there forever which seemed to give him a lot of pleasure because he became more passionate than ever. The heaving gasping urgency of him, the tight clasp of his hands on her shoulders, the feel of her breasts against his chest aroused her also to a point of climax she had only very rarely enjoyed before.

Twice if she remembered. George now made it three times.

She still had her legs tangled around him and his weight was on her, his heart pounding furiously. She lay in the dark looking out at the bright sky, with this handsome virile man on top of her and she felt very happy. She still squeezed with her legs and his penis gradually flopped out of her and lay in all the sticky wetness it had created between her thighs.

Fay thought it was incredible to feel such joy, such happiness and fulfilment, at something that had always disgusted her. This mess and the smell and the sweat had always given her nausea, made her sick, made her rush to the bathroom to wash herself thoroughly to try and get rid of all that awful stuff.

Why, now, she wanted just to stay here, not to move and to feel him against her. She wished it could last.

George Galbraith, who was as expert after love as he was during and before, was now gently kissing her face, her ears, her nose. It was important to make a woman feel appreciated, not just a thing. She could see his eyes in the gloom looking at her, his mouth smiling.

'Did you come?'

'Yes.'

'Good. You're fantastic, Fay.'

He gently rolled off her and wiped himself and her with some tissues from a box beside the bed. Then he got in beside her again and put his arm under her head. Oh he smelt lovely, soapy, clean, after-shave and warm. Fay snuggled up to him more. He had a wonderful body, no ounce of surplus flesh, no sagging bits. She couldn't help thinking of Lorna.

'I thought I was frigid after Jack,' Fay confided. 'I hated it.'

'Frigid? But you're superb. You're a natural. I must see you again and again and again, Fay – would you like to see me?'

'You mean become lovers?'

'We're lovers now. Go on being lovers.'

'But what about Lorna?'

George sighed. This was the part he never liked, because all the girls, except the ones abroad, asked this sooner or later.

'Well Lorna . . . Lorna has never been very sexy.'

'But you sleep in the same bed.'

'Yes, but hardly ever *together*, like this.'

'Hardly?'

'Well, once a year maybe, at Christmas.'

Fay giggled. 'You mean you're free?'

'Very.'

'But how can we?'

'I've been thinking about it,' George said. 'I think I could arrange something.'

'What sort of thing?'

'Well, get you away.'

'From here?'

'Yes.'

'This flat?'

'Yes.'

Fay sat up in bed, the bedclothes dropping from her leaving, above George's head, a lovely arc of firm, full breastline. Her right nipple was just by his mouth and he put out his tongue and began gently to lick around the nipple and then suck it.

'How can I get away from this flat?'

George freed his mouth. 'I could maybe get you another one. Some nice place like Knightsbridge.'

'They have council flats in Knightsbridge?'

'Oh no, not a council flat. No, my group has recently gone into property and I think I could manage something nice.'

'Are you joking?'

'It would be a cruel joke, wouldn't it? I'm perfectly serious. I'd like a steady girl-friend, a mistress if you like. I think you'd suit – if I suit you.'

'If *you* suit me? Her head swam with excitement, with desire again as his tongue gently caressed her navel, then flicked over her soft belly moving further down. The sensation was intense; he looked up to see if she was liking it, and satisfied by the way she wriggled and arched her back, he resumed his caress.

Jack had never done anything like this! Just leapt on her and stuck it in, hurting her, never even attempting to arouse her as George did, making her feel so sexy and wet with his tongue. Jack would have thought something like this was disgusting, and so would she, then, to be honest. But with George it was different. The very way he had eased her nervousness by talking to her and helping her off with her clothes, and then lying beside her on the bed, just stroking and kissing and lick-ing parts of her as though there was all the time in the world... Why, all this had just shown how practised, how sure and confident the man was compared to Jack. And it had helped her to relax and unwind and lose her nervousness and, yes, her shame, so that she had an urgent feeling of wanting to respond to him.

She could never imagine Jack having this leisurely approach to love-making, having the time and the care, no matter how many books he read on the subject. George made her feel an equal partner in making love; with Jack she was always an object.

Up here it was so light from the night sky it seemed like day and in the glow she could see the elongated shapes of her nipples, the heavy swell of her breasts silhouetted against George's eager face. She felt inspired to invent and improvise for him and she raised herself on her knees, balancing carefully astride his body. George gave a gasp of delighted satisfaction as she sank on to him, her breasts full and heavy, touching his chest; her face tender and aroused. As he grasped her smooth Rubensesque hips in both hands, adjusting himself to her rhythm, he was convinced that he had found the perfect answer to his problem; a refuge from home.

He wasn't quite sure when it had come to him as a positive idea. Of course Fay wasn't a stranger; it wasn't like a casual pick up. She was a family friend, an old friend of Lorna's anyway. Their children had known each other for years. It had all come to him at the dance really, and her subsequent willingness and expertise, despite what she said about not having made love for so long, not even liking it, which was nonsense, convinced him that here would be a nice permanent liaison, something he'd needed for some time. He'd had any amount of one-night stands, weekends, even weeks, but it was always someone different because he was always on the go.

Now with something permanent, a second wife really – the orientals were so sensible about this – he could settle down, become adjusted to his new job and the demands of his home.

Fay's face was ecstatic.

'Are you having another orgasm?'

'Yes.'

'Good, let it come, my darling. I can't just yet,' but he pressed her tenderly to him, her face in his neck, holding the trembling shuddering of her moving buttocks tightly to him, aching with the pleasure of her gripping thighs.

'There, you're a sexpot,' he said as she lay flat on his body, hearing now the thudding of her heart.

'I can't understand it. *Twice* so soon. I never thought I was capable . . .'

'You weren't aroused, you poor girl. You dear thing. Fay, I've been thinking seriously about this. I mean it. A flat in Knightsbridge. I'll keep you. All this behind you.'

'You mean I needn't work?'

'No, you'll be my mistress like in the old times. My second wife.'

'But can you afford it?'

'Oh, money's no problem.'

'But how will you fix it with Lorna?'

He looked at her with surprise, an expression she could not see in the dark.

'I won't tell Lorna. I'm not going to *live* with you. I mean not all the time. But I'll visit you a lot and stay on occasions. You see I can't leave Lorna and the children. I wouldn't want to and you wouldn't want me to either. Not after what Jack did, would you?'

'No,' doubtfully. 'But you're quite unlike Jack.'

'Yes, but we would have to be quite clear about this, darling. I would provide a home and an income; but I would never expect to marry you, not unless something happened to Lorna. Think about it. You needn't make up your mind now.'

'What about the children?'

'Well, Ralph's going to boarding school; maybe Quentin should go there too. Then you'd just have Amanda.'

'But what about the school?'

'Oh, they'd leave Princess Maud. I think it would be a good thing. Besides, if you moved out of the district you'd have no contact with Lorna. I really think that would be best,' he added delicately.

No more gas board. No more toiling up twenty flights of stairs when the lifts broke down or there was a power cut. No more rubbish jamming up in the shoot, panic wondering where the children were, how to get the doctor if they were ill because she had no telephone.

It would be a different life; a new world. A mistress.

* * *

Lorna was only vaguely aware that George had stayed out all night and only vaguely curious when he came in. The children were all clattering about in the kitchen eating breakfast in various stages. There were broken egg shells on the table and bits of rind on the floor. There were eggy faces and happy expressions, contented.

George was contented too. He smiled at his wife and pecked her on the cheek.

'Darling, did you only just come home?' she looked reproachful. 'What happened to Fay?'

'Oh, I took her home. Then I spent the night at a Turkish bath. I said I'd pick up the kids and take them back.'

Lorna disapproved of Turkish baths as a remnant of the Age of Imperialism, but George used them a lot; he said to escape from tension. He quite often stayed out at night at a Turkish bath.

'How sweet of you dear. You are kind, George. I'm out all day at the women's lib demo in Hyde Park. Could you, darling . . .?'

'Certainly, I'll look after everything.'

'Oh, I'm so glad to have you home, George, you're a pet.' She smiled gratefully at him in passing, the missing buttons from her stained, unbecoming pink gown showing the amplitude of bosom that had revolted George yesterday, but that somehow he didn't mind so much today.

Overnight George Galbraith had made himself a happy man and the best part about it was: he was going to make *everyone* else happy too – Fay and her children, and Lorna and theirs.

He went gaily upstairs to bath and shave, singing a song.

16

The Summer Fair dance had a peculiar aftermath for Alex Twentyman too, something that was to affect her and her family all her life, just as much as George's singular act of altruism was to affect his, and Fay's and Lorna's.

Alex and Itzhak too had left early, shortly after Fay and George. They were eager to be alone together. Carla and Milt remained with the dancers, entwined round each other in the manner of lovers, dancing a slow fox-trot.

Alex and Itzhak had hurried home and, just as George and Fay had done, and goodness knows how many other couples that warm Saturday night in July, they made love.

Only this time Alex had something on her mind. She and Itzhak had been making love regularly for three months and yet there was no suspicion of her being pregnant; she'd just finished the curse the day before.

Alex too was lying on her back in the dark, puzzling. When Itzhak grunted and put a large hand across her belly she said,

'Itzhak, are you awake?'

'Yes, darling.'

'Itzhak, I'm a bit puzzled about something.'

He leaned up on one elbow, alert. 'Something wrong?'

'Not at all. I'm so happy, you know that.'

'And I'm happy too, my darling.'

He cuddled up to her putting his head on her stomach – her beautiful slightly rounded stomach, ivory coloured. He could see the top of her pubic hairs. He could just pull the sheets back and see all of her if he liked. He, alone of all men, had that privilege with Alexandra Twentyman. He felt a wonderful feeling of possession; of owning something unique and marvellous. Yes, he did pull the bedclothes back, just because he could, and look at all of her, and himself very dark and big and hairy beside her.

'What are you doing?'

'Just comparing our bodies.'

Alex looked down and smiled, touched his arm, linked his hand with hers.

'Itzhak, you know I don't use any contraceptives?'

Pause. Itzhak frowned. 'No. Are you pregnant?'

'No, that's what puzzles me.'

He sat up and put his arms around his legs.

'Why didn't you use any contraceptives? I thought you had the Pill or the coil, or something like that.'

'No.'

'Did you do it deliberately?' He didn't sound angry, just curious.

'No. I went off the Pill after Harry left and never went on it again. It's supposed to get dangerous as you get older. I don't use anything else.'

'You shouldn't worry too much about getting pregnant,' Itzhak said. 'I didn't tell you because it didn't come up, but, well . . . that's partly why Hannah . . .'

'What, Itzhak?' Now she was alarmed by the expression on his face. Did he have a disease of some unmentionable sort?

'I'm sub-fertile. It's unlikely, but not impossible, mind you, that I'll ever be a father. Hannah wanted children so badly; she didn't want to wait and see.'

'Oh.'

Alex avoided his eyes. She felt terribly flat and let down. This wonderful tender man, whom she was beginning to be well and truly in love with, couldn't give her a child. She would now only ever have two children, supposing that she and Itzhak spent their lives together, which they were talking about. She would never, ever, complete the family she so much wanted. Never feel a new baby again in her arms.

'You're not disappointed. Are you, Alexandra?'

She looked at him and saw the fear, the pain in his eyes. Imagined the taunts from Hannah, the reduction of Itzhak's self-esteem. No wonder he'd been shy.

He hadn't told her because he'd been afraid. She loved him more for it, for all the hurt that he'd endured. She stretched beside him, lay on her stomach and began to kiss his face.

'Of course I'm not disappointed. I'm relieved, silly. I've got two children. Why ever should I want more?'

'Of course, there is a chance.'

But Alex knew it would never happen.

* * *

'And,' Emma Drax said with an air of magnanimity, 'I told Roger he could do what he liked about the house. Money is just of no interest to Charlie.'

'And what did Roger say?'

'He said he'd sell it and move into a flat. It's his house, of course, but it's the matrimonial home so I'm entitled to a share. Charlie said it's the least he could do for Roger. Let him sell the house and raise some money; keep his pride. Charlie is very thoughtful like that.'

'Are you going to marry him?'

Emma's eyes looked sharp, calculating. 'That I don't know. He hasn't asked me.'

'But isn't it taking a risk? Just moving out and living with Charlie?'

'Oh no. We're having an agreement, a settlement as it were. I'm not that daft. But oh you should see his home, just on the Surrey border. Acres of . . .'

It happened so quickly. Charlie and Emma had met when he came to pick his daughter up from the Draxes' house during a custodial visit Harriet was making to him. They'd talked for hours and had dinner together the same week.

'We just had *so* much in common. He loves golf and bridge and all the things I do. He's got such a *brain.* The Fleischman Corporation. You've heard of it, haven't you. *The* Fleischman Corporation. Mind you it might be nice to be Mrs Fleischman, maybe Lady Fleischman in time, I won't deny. But I'm not forcing him. He hasn't quite got over his divorce. It was a very bitter thing with a big legal wrangle. She had pots of money in her own right.'

'What did Roger say?'

'Poor Rog. He's had such a year. First the business and now me, and of course I'm taking Portia with me. Oh he couldn't possibly have her, even if he wanted to. He couldn't look after her or afford to send her to the convent. No question. I don't really feel sorry for Roger. He's the victim of his own weaknesses. Darling, I'm so pleased about you and Itzhak! He's not handsome, but so nice isn't he? Charlie's not handsome either – did you ever meet him? In fact he's plain ugly; but, well, that's not the most important thing is it? I can see you're so much happier with Itzhak, and so much more suited. Poor Harry. I don't think he's as . . .'

'Oh?' Alex said sharply not having consciously recalled Harry for some weeks. The affair with Itzhak, coinciding with Harry's wedding, had almost blotted him out of her mind. The children had been with their grandmother part of the summer, away at various camps, and also with Harry. She'd hardly seen him. She and Itzhak had travelled through Europe to Israel. It had been a heavenly holiday, the best she'd ever remembered. Now it was nearly time for school again and she'd come home leaving Itzhak to finish his work in Israel and follow her in a week or two.

'Harry isn't happy?'

'Oh I don't say he's not *happy*. He looks well enough. But he's certainly kept on a string by Rosalind. My goodness she never takes her eyes off him. It must be awfully constricting.'

* * *

It was. Harry had thought Rosalind would get over the possessive stage after they were married; she just didn't seem to trust him. When he did complain about it one embarrassing time when she'd stopped him dancing with an office colleague's wife she said well, after all, that was how she got him wasn't it? She was devastatingly logical that way.

Rosalind had Harry so well organized both at home and at work that he hardly had time to think; certainly he was never out of her sight. They shared an office, they attended meetings together, they ate together and they slept together. Occasionally they had different wine tasting sessions because Harry was an expert on Burgundies and wines of the Côtes du Rhône, while Rosalind's more delicate palate appreciated the soft wines of Germany and Alsace.

It was a bit much really. When Harry thought about it, in the few free moments he was ever allowed to think, he wondered why he'd let her organize his life so much, why he'd fallen into the trap? In the dim haze of memory he thought of Alex and the children and the rather happy, normal, *relaxed* life they'd shared together. Yes, it had a distinctly roseate glow now. Then why had he let Rosalind . . . He tried to cast his mind back, digging away at the little crevices of lapsed time.

Well, Alex had been rather boring; that really was what it came to. Compared to Rosalind, at the time anyway, he was not so sure about now, she was just an ordinary little housewife; pretty, yes; sexy, fairly, but not very adventurous – demanding actually, but passive. Sex to her had been something that he 'did' while she just lay there and enjoyed herself. It had been quite exhausting at times, all that effort on a pretty, supine body.

Now Rosalind had been around a great deal when she'd met him and the most important thing at the beginning was the utterly exciting, different things Rosalind could get up to in bed. Quite normal now, it had seemed incredible at the time after all those faithful years with Alex. That had really lured him from Alex, and then, of course, Rosalind had gradually taken over in every compartment of his life.

Now she was usually rather tired at nights. Well, they both were. The children were chattering in the back of the car, Harry ruminating on his way back from Putney. He was returning them to their mother after the holiday. And what a fuss Rosalind had made of *that*! You'd have thought she had been asked to look after them for a whole year.

'Spoiling our holiday, Harry,' she'd said.

'But darling we have all our lives together.'

'Yes but the *Tyrol* with *two* children! Not quite what I expected.'

Then he got angry.

'Sweetheart we had a whole month in Majorca for our honeymoon. Is it too much to ask? To give Alex a break?'

Yes it was etc. etc. etc. However the holiday had not been such a disaster because the children had had a very good time, met lots of other kids, and Rosalind had only sulked for a day or two. He thought she resented the idea of appearing the least bit maternal; but really the kids had taken to her and she now couldn't pretend not to like them, a bit anyway.

'Well, your mother's back from Israel, I hear.'

'With Itzhak.'

Harry's heart sank. He had spent a good deal of the holiday hearing about Itzhak, Alex's new boyfriend. How he was so good at making things and doings things and taking them on the heath. He kept them, it seemed, constantly amused, entertained, and even instructed. Why he even got their meals if Alex wanted a night out. Such a scene of domesticity conjured itself up that Harry almost began to feel jealous. In fact he was sure he wouldn't like Itzhak at all. He was curious to find out.

The children were overjoyed to be home and see their mother again. They flung themselves into her arms and her eyes filled with tears. But oh, they looked so happy and yes, Toby had grown even taller.

'Oh Mummy, it was wonderful. Austria . . .'

'And Gran said . . .'

'And there was this otter . . .'

'I can't wait to see . . .'

Then they rushed upstairs to their rooms leaving chaos in the hall downstairs.

Harry couldn't stop staring at Alex. She almost looked like a different person, she'd changed so much. Why she even seemed to have *grown.* It was ridiculous because of course she hadn't, couldn't have . . . but she held herself differently. Her breasts seemed to protrude in a sexy way he was sure they never had before. Her hair was more attractively arranged; her buttocks rounder.

'How have you been, Alex? You look well.'

'Oh, we've had a marvellous summer. Thank you so much for taking the children. Mind you, I've missed them. Did Rosalind . . .?'

'Oh, not at all. She's rather fond of them.'

'Maybe she'll change her mind about having her own.'

Harry studied the toes of his elegant suede shoes. He'd been playing golf that day.

'Oh no. She's quite firm about that.' He looked at his watch. 'Alex, would you like me to help you put the kids to bed?

It's late for them. They've had supper.'

Alex couldn't quite believe it was Harry Twentyman speaking. Marriage to Rosalind had done him good. In the old days Harry always studied the evening paper over a glass of whisky while she gave the kids their baths and cooked the dinner. It never occurred to him to offer to help. An occasional variation when she hadn't felt well perhaps.

'That's very kind of you, Harry. I think they'd like that. Have you eaten?'

'Well . . .'

He looked at her and she looked at him. Yes, he still charmed her; that rueful smile, the glimmer of excitement in his eyes.

'I hoped I'd meet . . . er?'

'Itzhak? He's still in Israel. Back next week. I hope.'

'Well, I'm glad for you, Alex.'

'Thank you, Harry.'

They moved into the sitting room, shoulders almost touching as they pressed at the same time through the door.

'Very glad the kids like him. Glad that you've got a man. Delighted, really I am.'

He moved over to the sideboard and poured himself a drink. Now that he no longer maintained her – the money went entirely for the children's benefit, Itzhak had insisted on that, and she made quite a good income of her own typing and doing bits of research Itzhak put her way – she thought he had a nerve helping himself to the whisky. In fact Harry still felt he lived here, she decided. Part owned the place, which in fact he did. That much was true.

'Harry I've only got some cold chicken . . .'

'That would be *marvellous*,' Harry said with instant enthusiasm, as though she'd mentioned caviare. 'Anything in the cellar. The odd bottle still?'

'I expect so.'

She laughed. He laughed. He looked vigorous and excited and downed his whisky in a gulp.

'I'll just rush up and speed those kids to bed. See if we've got any of the Beaune '69 left, darling. Decant it carefully.' He took off his jacket as he went out and rolled up his sleeves.

'We've got', 'darling'. Yes Harry still felt he lived here. No doubt about that. Well, he did belong here in a way. They'd been married for twelve years; the children upstairs were theirs. Flesh of their flesh. You couldn't help feeling very fond of Harry still, even if you knew you were free of him, in love with Itzhak. You couldn't make all those years just fade out.

Besides, she was in the middle of her cycle. Just the right time for conception.

* * *

'Do you forgive me, Alex?'

'For this?'

'Oh no, darling, I don't mean *this*. I know you enjoyed it and so did I. No, for the way I left. It was a ghastly thing to do. I can't seem to visualize the kind of heel I must have been.'

'I suppose I was to blame too, Harry. I've only recently seen myself as I must have been.'

'How, darling?'

Her figure had filled out too; her breasts *were* larger, and her technique . . . amazing, hardly the same woman he'd made love to for twelve years. Well, it just showed that she hadn't been around enough. If she had, things might have been very different.

'Well, dull.'

'Never.'

'Yes, I was dull. The little housewife waiting for you to come home. I must have bored you to death.'

'Oh no, not at all. I'm the one to blame and I shall never forgive myself for the agony I caused you. Never.'

He kissed her lingeringly on the mouth. Maybe just again to make sure, Alex thought, lying back and spreading her legs open invitingly. Harry was aware of her movement, her desire, and excited by it. She really did want him, and how she turned him on! It was a bit soon but, oh well, try and summon up the beast again and, as the beast obediently started to rise, he guiltily thought of Rosalind waiting for him at home. It was a wonder the phone hadn't rung already. Still it was quite early. The kids had been tired and gone straight to sleep. He'd say he'd stopped in at the pub if she asked. She was sure to ask.

It had been a lovely two hours with Alex. Fun, too, for being somehow illicit, making love to your own ex-wife. With any luck they'd be able to make quite a thing of it, once in a while when he brought the children home.

17

Alex stood in the school playground looking up at the Victorian gables of Princess Maud School, the sun shining on the new white paint as it had over a year ago. It was a beautiful day, late November, and the gulls were wheeling about in the sky, a few leaves still on the trees in the streets. It was a clear sky, cerulean, somehow mediterranean.

How she loved the school now, how happy she was. How very different from that time when the kids had first started here. And what a lot of things seemed to have happened; she'd lost a husband and gained a lover – a man she respected and now adored. You couldn't help loving Itzhak because not only was he kind and thoughtful, as Harry had never been, but he was vulnerable too. She felt more equality with him than she'd ever felt with Harry.

And the kids had settled down, looked forward to their new term. Having Itzhak helped there too; he provided them with a solid father figure replacing the casual visits of Harry; though not so casual really, because Harry always seemed to think that she'd go to bed with him again and he hung round for as long as he could until she almost had to turn him out. Harry never understood why they had never recaptured the rapport of that night. He looked hurt about it every time.

Alex put a hand on her stomach. No movement yet, it was much too early, but she was sure. The pregnancy test was good and positive. She felt a great sense of satisfaction at being pregnant again and turned towards the gate. Carla was flying along the playground tugging Franco by the hand.

'Hurry, you'll be late. Alex! Hey wait!'

Alex watched Carla urging Franco upstairs and leaned against the wall, her hands in her pockets. She didn't feel at all guilty about what she'd done, making Harry impregnate her. After all, he was her ex-husband and he owed her something for all the misery he'd caused. He would never know the baby was his and Itzhak was overjoyed to think he'd fathered a child; so his virility had been restored to him. Maybe he *had* fathered it; you could never be really sure and he'd come back unexpectedly soon after she'd been to bed with Harry. It was a comfort to think of that. But in her heart she felt it was Harry's; she knew it was.

Anyway unless the child looked like her and was blond like Toby there shouldn't be any other striking difference, because Itzhak and Harry did have that slight resemblance, everyone had commented on it.

Carla ran out of the building over to Alex, her face alight with pleasure.

'Alex I've just heard! You're getting married.'

Alex smiled. 'Well, yes. Not immediately but eventually. It's a badly kept secret, I'm afraid. I suppose Lorna told you.'

'Yes, Itzhak told her. He couldn't keep the reason for it to himself. And you must be thrilled to be having a baby.'

'I am.'

'It's what you've always wanted.'

'Yes.'

'Maybe you'll have the four you planned.'

'Oh I wouldn't be too sure about that. Maybe just the one more. I'm getting old, you know. Anyway, no Open University for the time being.'

'Does Harry know?'

'Not yet. It's not really his business is it? How's Milt?'

They were walking towards the gate, companionable, keeping stride. Carla went on walking but didn't speak. Alex felt a frisson of alarm. She wanted everyone to be happy like her.

'Milt's going back to the States. His company have sent for him.'

'Oh Carla.'

They stopped and looked at each other. Carla showed her emotions so visibly; now she was pale and tired-looking, as she had been before the advent of Milt.

'Yes, it's sad.'

'But won't you . . .?'

Carla shook her head. 'Marry him? No. He wants me to, but after living with him I've made up my mind. It won't work. It's not only the age gap; it's everything. He is just a kid, and a wealthy spoilt kid. He gets into terrible tantrums if he doesn't have his own way. I can take a bit of it, but not for the rest of my life. I'm too independent. I think that's why he was so strongly attracted to me; it's my age as well as everything else. He does want a mother basically.

'We've had a wonderful affair, and I'm grateful for it. But, no. Besides he and Franco don't get on and that's important. He isn't mature enough to deal with Franco's natural jealousy, and they have awful rows. Even if I sent Franco to boarding school I don't think it would solve the problem; there would still be the holidays. And Franco would feel I was putting him away and resent it, maybe for the rest of his life. No, it's over.'

Carla smiled at Alex but Alex could still see how much she was suffering. It must have been a hard decision. Milt had a lot of money and Carla liked money; he could have kept her in comfort for the rest of her life.

'How will you manage?'

'Well, there's always the massage parlour!' Seeing the look on Alex's face Carla laughed. 'I said that to shock you and I did. It wasn't too hard, you know. O.K. so I was corrupted; I also learned a lot about life. No, for the time being anyway, I thought I'd divide the house; sell the other half to raise a bit of capital. I don't want to spend my life as a high class tart unless I have to and then, you know, I'll soon get another man. I always do. Maybe a wealthy and wise one this time.'

Carla gave the soft sensuous laugh Alex so admired; but then she admired Carla altogether. Someone who could make out, as Alex never would.

'Franco must come to tea soon. I'll ring you, and Carla, count on us if you want anything. When Milt goes back, you know? It will be hard.'

'I know, Alex. Lorna said the same thing. You're good friends. I miss Fay, don't you?'

Alex frowned.

'I do and I don't. I was fond of Fay and we grew pretty intimate; but I always felt she never really lost the slight hostility she initially felt towards me. I mean she was prickly;

if she could jab in a point about my looks, or the way I walked or where I lived, she would. She was always so desperately suspicious and insecure that the barrier she erected never completely came down. Anyway I've got to know a lot more people now, and she was never as much my friend as you and Lorna.'

'Do you know Freda Ullthorne, Mary Ullthorne's mother? She's very nice. Mary's coming for tea tomorrow. They live just near us, the Ullthornes. They seem a very happy pleasant family. Itzhak and I are invited for dinner.'

Carla smiled.

'Itzhak and you. Now that you're no longer on your own, you'll only know happy, well-adjusted couples like you.'

'Nonsense, Carla, the old complacent Alex has gone forever. I'll never be as I was again. I'll never want to. Isn't life funny how things change so much in a short time? You, me, Fay . . . I wonder if we'll ever see her again? Have you seen her since she moved to Knightsbridge?'

'Me? No. She just upped and went during the summer holidays. It seemed as though she didn't want any of her old friends to know. It was all very mysterious. As though she wanted to cut out the past.'

'That I can understand.' Alex said. 'Someone wanting to make a fresh start. But how? Why? No one knows, do they?'

'I think *someone* knows, if you ask me.'

'Oh? Who?'

'You remember the Summer Fair dance?'

'You mean . . . George Galbraith? Surely not.'

'I happen to know his company has expanded and acquired a lot of property in Knightsbridge. One of his fellow directors is a patient of mine; he dislocated his hip in the summer. He never says anything, he's too discreet, but it's my guess George was beind Fay's sudden move.'

'But Lorna . . . she doesn't know?'

'Of course she doesn't. She's very hurt with Fay. Says she doesn't know how she could move without telling her, or saying goodbye, because she and George were always so kind to Fay.'

'That is Lorna's trouble of course. She does like to be thanked. Well I never. So you think George . . . my goodness. Maybe he taught Fay how to like sex at last.'

'It would be the security that would attract Fay, never mind sex. I think I'll try and get in touch with her. I'd love to know the truth.'

The truth. Alex wondered if you ever knew the truth about people. Wasn't it just a series of disconnected little parts? For instance if this was the truth about George Galbraith, that he kept a mistress in a luxurious flat in Knightsbridge, it astonished her. How could he square it with his socialist principles, his chairmanship of the local Labour Party? And if Lorna knew about it, were to find out, what price women's true liberation then? How would she feel?

'I feel sorry for Lorna if it is true; in a way, though, I suppose we never know the whole truth there either, about the Galbraiths. Talking about Lorna, we have another committee . . .'

They both consulted diaries, ringed dates and promised to phone each other. Then they pecked cheeks and made for their own small cars. Carla to her treatment rooms and Alex to . . . well, plan for the baby and the wedding. She wasn't quite sure which would come first. She didn't mind.

The last two years had taught Alex Twentyman that you couldn't reach any final conclusions about life. It ought to be nice and rounded, but it wasn't. So that which came first, the baby or the wedding, didn't matter.

Also available from Mandarin Paperbacks

NICOLA THORNE

The Perfect Wife and Mother

The price of freedom

To her friends, Ruth Harrow is the perfect wife to a loving husband and the devoted mother to three intelligent children. She alone knows the cost of motherhood.

Then the Lazars move in next door, and Ruth, compelled to re-evaluate her role, decides to return to college. But when Anton Lazar awakens in her a smouldering passion she has never known, her desire for freedom and another man rages out of all control . . .

'A wry, perceptive novel'

Irish Times

'Nicola Thorne is funny, shrewd and totally uncompromising'

Selena Hastings

FIONA HILL

The Stanbroke Girls

At Six Stones, Lady Emilia has good reason to be vexed by her intransigent brother. For Lord Marchmont is a bachelor who is as aloof as he is eligible. And he must marry and produce an heir – or one day forfeit his estates to his raffish cousin, Sir Jeffery de Guere.

The climate at Haddon House, Grosvenor Square, could not be more cheerful. As winter defers to the oncoming season of balls and invitations, the Stanbroke Girls – the dreamy and beautiful Lady Isabella, and her intelligent and even more exquisite sister Lady Elizabeth – are at the centre of their elegant circle.

So when Lord Marchmont at last becomes a little more gallant than is his wont, no one could be happier than Lady Emilia. But an unexpected intrusion from the rake in their family engenders some dramatic complications.

'Considerably more wit and pizazz than the legendary Georgette Heyer herself'

Kirkus

Hill is 'in excellent twig' in her latest Regency romance . . . (she) interjects tongue-in-cheek asides to keep afloat the good humour of this frothy romance'

Publishers Weekly